Natalia Ginzburg

Happiness, as Such

Translated from the Italian
by Minna Zallman Proctor

A NEW DIRECTIONS PAPERBOOK

Originally published in Italian as *Caro Michele* in 1973. Published by arrange-
ment with the Estate of Natalia Ginzburg and Giulio Einaudi Editore SpA

Manufactured in the United States of America
New Directions Books are printed on acid-free paper
First published as a New Directions Paperbook (NDP1449) in 2019

Library of Congress Cataloging-in-Publication Data
Names: Ginzburg, Natalia, author. | Proctor, Minna, translator.
Title: Happiness, as Such / Natalia Ginzburg ; translated by Minna Zallman
Proctor.
Other titles: Caro Michele. English
Description: New York : New Directions, 2019. | "A New Directions Book."
Identifiers: LCCN 2019004328 | ISBN 9780811227995 (alk. paper)
Subjects: LCSH: Young men—Family relationships—Fiction. | Families—
Fiction.
Classification: LCC PQ4817.I5 C313 2019 | DDC 853/.912—dc23
LC record available at https://lccn.loc.gov/2019004328

10 9 8 7 6 5 4 3

New Directions Books are published for James Laughlin
by New Directions Publishing Corporation
80 Eighth Avenue, New York 10011

About Natalia Ginzburg

"Ginzburg never raises her voice, never strains for effect, never judges her creations. Like Chekhov, she knows how to stand back and let her characters expose their own lives, their frailties and strengths, their illusions and private griefs. The result is nearly translucent writing—writing so clear, so direct, so seemingly simple that it gives the reader the magical sense of apprehending the world for the first time."
   —Michiko Kakutani, *The New York Times*

"If Ferrante is a friend, Ginzburg is a mentor."
   —*The Guardian*

"Her prose style is deceptively simple and very complex. Its effect on the reader is both calming and thrilling—that's not so easy to do."
   —Deborah Levy

"I'm utterly entranced by Ginzburg's style—her mysterious directness, her salutary ability to lay things bare that never feels contrived or cold, only necessary, honest, clear."
   —Maggie Nelson

"Ginzburg gives us a new template for the female voice and an idea of what it might sound like. This voice emerges from her preoccupations and themes, whose specificity and universality she considers with a gravitas and authority that seem both familiar and entirely original."
   —Rachel Cusk

Happiness, as Such

By NATALIA GINZBURG

FROM NEW DIRECTIONS

The Dry Heart

Happiness, as Such

Happiness, as Such

1

A WOMAN AWOKE in her new house. Her name was Adriana. It was snowing out, and her birthday, she was forty-three years old. The house was in the country. The village was visible from the house, on a hilltop, two kilometers away. Fifteen kilometers to the city. Adriana had moved in ten days earlier. She pulled on a light, tobacco-brown robe. Slid her long, narrow feet into a pair of slippers that were also tobacco-brown and trimmed with dirty white fur. She headed to the kitchen and made a cup of instant coffee to dunk biscuits in. There were apple peels on the table and she swept them into a newspaper to keep for the rabbits they didn't have yet but would soon because the milkman had promised to bring them. Then she went into the living room and pulled open the shutters. She saw herself in the mirror hanging over the sofa. She was tall, she wore her wavy copper hair cropped short, she had a small head and a long strong neck, her green eyes were wide-set and sad. She sat down at the desk to write a letter to her only son.

Dear Michele, she wrote, I'm writing primarily to tell you that your father is sick. Go visit him. He says he hasn't seen you for days. I was there yesterday. It was the first Thursday of the month, and I was waiting for him at Canova's Tea Shop when I got a call from his butler telling me he was ill. So I went on up. He was in bed. Seemed quite worn out. There were bags under his eyes and his skin looked awful. He has painful indigestion and isn't eating anything. Naturally, he's still smoking.

When you go see him, don't bring your usual twenty-five pairs of dirty socks. The butler, I can't remember if his name is Enrico or Federico, isn't up to the extra burden of managing your dirty laundry right now. He's exhausted and overwhelmed. He doesn't sleep at night because your father keeps calling for him. And it's the first time he's ever been a butler. He was a mechanic before. Plus, he's an idiot.

If you have a lot of dirty laundry, you can bring it here. I have a woman helping me, Cloti. She started five days ago. She's not very nice. She's always scowling and things with her are already shaky, so if you were to show up with a suitcase full of laundry to wash and iron, that would be just fine. I should remind you however that there are good laundromats near your studio and you're old enough to take care of yourself. You'll be twenty-two soon. Speaking of which, it's my birthday. The twins gave me new slippers. But I'm fond of my old slippers. I also wanted to tell you that it would be a great improvement if you washed your socks and handkerchiefs at night instead of balling them up and leaving them to fester for weeks under your bed, but I've always told you that and the message has never gotten across.

I waited there for the doctor. He's Dr. Povo. Maybe Covo. I didn't quite catch his name. He lives in the building. I was unable to understand exactly what he thinks your father has. He says there's an ulcer, which we already know about. He says your father should go to a clinic but your father won't hear of it. I wonder if you think I should move into your father's house to help him. I think the same thing periodically but I won't do it. Sick people frighten me. I'm scared of other people's diseases, though I'm not scared of my own. But I've never really been seriously ill. I went to Holland when my father had diverticulitis. I knew perfectly well it wasn't diverticulitis. It was cancer. So I wasn't there when he died, which I regret. But after a certain point in life a person has to dunk her regrets in the morning coffee, just like biscuits.

Moreover, if I were to show up there with all my bags tomorrow, I don't know what your father would think. He's grown shy around me in the last few years. And I'm getting shy around him. There's nothing worse than shyness between two people who've hated each other. There's nothing to say. They can be grateful that they're not scratching and clawing at each other but that kind of gratitude hardly leads to dialogue. After we split up, your father and I started our dull but civilized routine of meeting each other for tea at Canova's the first Thursday of every month. I never cared for it and neither did he. His cousin Lillino, the lawyer, had suggested it—he always listens to his cousin Lillino, the lawyer from Mantua. According to Lillino the two of us needed to maintain a good relationship and meet regularly to discuss common concerns. The hours spent at Canova's have been torture for the both of us. Your father, who is methodical in his disorganization, had determined that we should remain sitting together at that table from five to seven thirty. Every so often he'd sigh loudly and look at his watch. That was humiliating, the way he stretched back in his chair and scratched at his mop of black hair. He reminds me of a tired old panther. We talked about you children. But he didn't care about your sisters. You are his light. From the moment you came into the world he got it stuck in his head that you are the only person in the world worthy of his kindness and praise. We talked about you, even though he's well aware

5

I don't understand you at all and that he is the only one who really knows you. And so that was the end of that conversation. The two of us are so worried about disagreeing that we avoid any conceivably volatile topic. You've always known about our afternoon meetings, but I don't think you knew that it was his damned cousin who advised us to have them. I realize that I'm talking about it as if we were still going to be meeting. In reality, I think your father is very sick and we won't ever meet again at Canova's on the first Thursday of the month.

If you weren't such a fool I'd tell you to move out of the studio and go back to Via San Sebastianello. You could be the one waking up all night instead of that butler. Realistically you don't actually do anything. Viola is running her household. Angelica works and has the baby. The twins are in school and are still young. Not to mention the fact that your father can't stand the twins. He can't stand Viola or Angelica either. He can't stand his own sisters either. Cecilia is old anyway and he and Matilde hate each other. Matilde is staying here now and will be here all winter. You're the only person who your father loves and can stand being around. But you aren't going to change, and I understand it's better if you stay put, in the studio. If you went to your father's house you'd just add to the confusion and drive the butler to despair.

Another thing I wanted to tell you. I got a letter from a person who says that her name is Mara Castorelli and that we met last year at a party at your studio. I remember the party but there were so many people that I can't remember anyone in particular. The letter went to my old address on Via dei Villini. This woman is asking me to help her find work. She wrote me from a boardinghouse that she needs to leave because it's too expensive. She says she has a baby that she would like to bring here so that I can meet him, this beautiful baby. I haven't answered her yet. I used to like babies but I have no desire at all to marvel over this baby. I'm too tired. I'd like you to tell me who this girl is and what kind of work she might be looking for because she doesn't explain it well in the letter. At first I didn't think much about the letter but then I started to wonder if the baby is yours. Because otherwise I don't understand why this woman would have written. Her handwriting is crazy. I asked your father if he knew about this Martorelli woman friend of yours and he said he didn't and then he started talking about the Pastorella cheese that he likes to take with him when he goes out sailing. It's impossible to have a reasonable conversation with your father anymore. Gradually I've gotten it stuck in my mind that this baby is yours. Last night after dinner I went to pull out the car—the car is always such a drag to pull out—so that I could drive up to the village to call you but you're never home. While I was coming back I started to cry. In part I was thinking about your father who is so sick and in part I was thinking about you. If this Martorelli baby is yours, what will you do, you don't know how to do anything. You didn't finish school did you. I don't think your paintings of owls and falling-down buildings are that good. Your father says they are and that I don't understand painting. They look to me like the paintings your father did when he was young, but not as good. I don't know. Please tell me what I should say to this Martorelli and if I need to send her money. She hasn't asked but I'm sure that's what she wants.

I still don't have a telephone. I don't know how many times I've gone in to petition for service but no one ever comes. Will you do me the favor of going to the telephone company too. It's not much to ask because it's near you. Perhaps your friend

Osvaldo, who got you the studio, knows someone? The twins think that Osvaldo has a relation who works for the phone company. Can you find out if that's true. It was nice of him to give you the studio rent free, but it's too dark in there to paint. Maybe that's why you keep painting owls, because you have to keep the light on all the time and it always seems like night-time. That basement must be damp. Thank goodness I bought you a wood stove.

I doubt you'll come over for my birthday because I don't think you'll have remembered it. Neither Viola nor Angelica are coming, they can't make it, I talked to both of them on the phone yesterday. I'm pleased with this house but it is inconvenient to be so far from everyone. I thought the air out here would be good for the twins, but they're off first thing in the morning. Off to school on their mopeds. They eat in a pizzeria in town. They go to a friend's house to study and aren't home until after dark. I worry until they get home because I don't like them out on the road when it's dark. Your Aunt Matilde arrived three days ago. She wants to visit your father but he doesn't want to see her. They haven't gotten along for years. I wrote and asked Matilde to come because she was at her wits end and short on money. She'd made a bad investment in Switzerland. I asked her to tutor the twins a little. But the twins keep avoiding her. I will have to be there for her but I can hardly bear being around her.

I might have been wrong to buy this house. Sometimes I think it was a mistake. They are supposed to be bringing rabbits. When they get here, I'd like for you to come and build a cage. In the meantime I was thinking I could put them in the woodshed. The twins want a horse.

The main reason for moving, I think, was that I didn't want

to keep running into Filippo. He lived so close to Via dei Villini and I ran into him all the time. It was excruciating. He's
well. His wife is having a baby next spring. Good God, why do
all these babies keep coming when everyone is so fed up with
them and no one wants them around. There are just too many
babies.

I'll stop here. I need to give this letter to Matilde who's going
out shopping now and I'll stay here to watch the snow and read
Pascal's *Pensées*.

Your mother

The letter finished and tucked into an envelope, she went back
down to the kitchen. She greeted and kissed her fourteen-year-
old twins, Bebetta and Nannetta, with their identical blonde
braids, identical blue jackets bearing their school insignia, and
identical knee socks, who left for school on identical mopeds.
She greeted and kissed her sister-in-law, Matilde, a fat mannish
spinster with straight white hair, one lock always falling over
her eyes so that she'd have to brush it away with a haughty
gesture. There was no trace of Cloti, the maid. Matilde wanted
to summon her, noting that every morning she woke up fifteen
minutes later and was always complaining about her lumpy
mattress. Cloti finally appeared, slinking down the hallway,
wearing a sky-blue dressing gown, short and fluffy, her long
grey hair loose around her shoulders. She went into the bathroom and reappeared wearing a starched brown apron. Her
hair was smoothed back with barrettes. She started making the
beds, tugging on the covers with enormous ennui, dramatiz-
ing with every gesture her desire to be fired. Matilde put on a
Tyrolese cape and announced that she was going on foot to do
the shopping, praising the icy fresh air and snow in her deep,

forceful voice. She instructed Cloti to boil several onions from the ones that were hanging in the kitchen. She had a good recipe for onion soup. Cloti answered in a weary voice that all the onions were rotten.

Adriana had gotten dressed and was now wearing tobacco-brown trousers and a beige sweater. She sat in the living room by the lit fire but she didn't read Pascal's *Pensées*. She didn't read anything and she didn't watch the snow out the window because suddenly she felt like she hated that snowy landscape with its shapes. Instead she put her head in her hands and then rubbed her feet and calves through the thick tobacco-brown socks and that's where she spent the whole morning.

2

A MAN NAMED Osvaldo Ventura entered a boardinghouse in Piazza Annibaliano. He was square, stocky, and wore a raincoat. His hair was grey-blond, his skin flushed pink, his eyes yellow. He tended to smile when he felt uncertain.

He'd gotten a telephone call from a girl he knew who was staying there. Someone had loaned her an apartment on Via dei Prefetti and she'd asked him for a ride.

She was waiting in the lobby, wearing a cotton turquoise shirt, eggplant-colored pants, and a black kimono with silver dragons embroidered on it. At her feet there were suitcases, shopping bags, and a baby in a plastic yellow bassinet.

"I've been sitting here for an hour like an idiot," she said.

Osvaldo gathered her things and started toward the door.

"You see that curly-haired lady by the elevator?" she asked. "She was in the next room over. She was nice to me. I owe her a lot. Money as well. Smile." Osvaldo smiled uncertainly at the curly-haired lady.

"This is my brother. He's here to pick me up. I'm going home. I'll bring back your thermos and everything else tomorrow," said Mara. She gave the curly-haired lady a kiss on each cheek.

Osvaldo picked the bags and bassinet back up and they left.

"I'm your brother?" he said.

"She was very nice. I told her you were my brother. Nice people like to meet relatives."

"Do you owe her a lot of money?"

"Not much. Do you want to pay her back?"

"No," said Osvaldo.

"I told her I'd bring it tomorrow. But that's a lie. I'll never come back to this place. I'll wire it to her one day."

"When?"

"When I find a job."

"What about the thermos?"

"I might not return the thermos. She has two."

Osvaldo's Fiat was parked across the square. It was snowing out and the wind was blowing. Mara held her big black felt hat on her head. She was a tiny, pale brunette, broad hipped, and very thin. Her dragon kimono blew in the wind and her sandals sunk into the snow.

"Don't you have anything warmer to wear?" he said.

"No. All my stuff is packed away in a trunk. Two friends on Via Cassia are holding it for me."

"Elisabetta is in the car," he said.

"Who's Elisabetta?"

"My daughter."

Elisabetta was curled up in the back seat. She was nine. She had carrot-colored hair and was wearing a checked sweater and matching top. She held a dog in her arms. The dog had long ears and tawny fur. They put the yellow bassinet on the seat next to her.

"How come you brought along this child and that animal?" said Mara.

"I had to pick Elisabetta up from her grandmother's," he said.

"You always have something to do. You do favors for every-one. You need to get your own life," she said.

"What makes you think I don't have a life?" he said.

"Hold on to that dog, Elisabetta. Make sure it doesn't lick my baby. Got it?" she said.

"How old is the baby now?" asked Osvaldo.

"He's twenty-two days old. Don't you remember? I left the hospital two weeks ago. The head nurse there was the one who told me about this boardinghouse. But I had to get out. It was filthy. I didn't want to step on the bathmat with my bare feet. It was one of those green rubber mats. You know how repulsive those green hotel bathmats can get."

"Yes, I know."

"And it cost too much. And they were rude. I need people to be kind. I've always needed that, but even more so now that I have a baby."

"I get it."

"Don't you need people to be kind, too?"

"Very much so."

"They said I rang down too often. I rang because there were so many things I needed. Like boiling water. And other things. I need to mix formula. It's very complicated. You have to weigh the baby, feed him, then weigh him again to see if he needs more milk. I would ring ten times and they would never come. When they would finally bring the boiling water I always wondered if it had actually been boiled."

"You could have gotten a kettle for your room."

"No, they didn't allow that. Then they always forgot something. The fork."

"What fork?"

"To mix the powdered milk. I told them to bring a bowl, a glass, a fork, and a spoon. Every time. They'd bundle it all in a tablecloth. The fork was always missing. So I'd ask for a fork again. A boiled clean fork. And then they'd be rude about it. There were times I considered asking them to boil the tablecloth too. But I worried they might throw a fit."

"I agree. They probably would have thrown a fit."

"I'd have to go to the curly-haired lady's room to weigh the baby. That lady you met. She has a baby and a baby scale. But then she very politely told me I shouldn't be coming to her room at two in the morning. So at night I had to improvise. I just don't know. Does your wife, perhaps, have one of those scales at home?"

"Elisabetta, is there a baby scale back at the house?" asked Osvaldo.

"I don't know. I don't think so," said Elisabetta.

"Everyone has one of those scales in the closet," said Mara.

"I don't think we do," said Elisabetta.

"But I need a scale."

"You can rent one at the pharmacy," said Oswaldo.

"What can I rent without money?"

"What kind of work are you looking for?" he asked.

"I don't know. Maybe I can work in your store, selling books."

"No. That won't do."

"Why not?"

"It's a hole in the wall. And I already have someone helping me out."

"I've met her. She's a cow."

"Signora Peroni. She used to be Ada's nanny. Ada my wife."

"Call me Peroni. *I'll* be your beer. Actually, wait—I'll be your cow …"

14

They came to a little piazza with a fountain in Trastevere. Elisabetta and the dog got out.

"Goodbye, Elisabetta," said Osvaldo.

Elisabetta disappeared into the doorway of a red building. She was gone.

"She barely said a word," Mara said.

"She's shy."

"Shy and rude. She didn't even look at the baby. It was as if he weren't there. I don't like the color of your house."

"That's not my house. That's where my wife and Elisabetta live. I live alone"

"I know. I forgot. You're always talking about your wife so I forget you live alone. Actually, give me your phone number. I just have the store number. What if I need something at night."

"I'd rather you didn't call me at night. I have trouble sleeping."

"You never let me come over to your house. When I ran into you on the street this summer and I had a stomach out to here and I said I wanted to take a shower, you told me there was no water."

"That was true."

"I was staying at a nunnery and we were only allowed to shower on Sundays."

"How did you end up at a nunnery?"

"It was cheap. I was staying on Via Cassia before that. Then I had a fight with my friends. They got mad at me for breaking their movie camera. They told me to go back to my family in Novi Ligure. They even gave me money to pay for the trip. They weren't cruel. But what was I supposed to do in Novi Ligure? I haven't spoken to those relatives in a long time. If they saw me come in with that giant belly they would have keeled over dead. And there are so many of them there and they don't have any money. But he's better than she is."

"He, who?"

"The husband. From Via Cassia. His wife is too obsessed with money. He's nice. He works for the television company. He told me that as soon as the baby came I could have a job. Maybe I should call him."

"Why maybe?"

"Because he asked me if I knew English and I told him I did. But I was lying. I don't know a word of English."

The apartment on Via dei Prefetti was comprised of three connecting rooms. In the back room there was a glass door with tattered curtains. The door opened onto a balcony that looked out onto a courtyard. There was a clothesline on the balcony and a faded lilac flannel nightgown was hanging on the line.

"The clothesline is very convenient," said Mara.

"Whose nightgown is that?" asked Osvaldo.

"Not mine. I've never been here before. The apartment belongs to a girl I know. She's not using it. I don't know whose nightgown that is. But it's not hers because she doesn't wear flannel to bed. She doesn't even wear nightgowns. She sleeps in the nude. She read somewhere that Finns sleep in the nude and it makes them strong."

"You didn't look at the apartment before taking it?"

"Of course not. It's a loan. I'm not paying for it. My good friend is lending me her apartment."

There was a round table in the back room, covered with a red-and-white checked oilcloth, and a queen-sized bed with a faded lilac-colored coverlet. In the middle of the room there was a hot plate, a sink, a broom, a wall calendar, and pots and plates piled on the ground. The front room was empty.

"You start boiling," she said. "There should be everything I need here. They told me there would be everything. A bowl. A cup. A fork. A spoon."

"I don't see any forks," said Osvaldo.

"Jesus Christ! I'm cursed when it comes to forks. I'll just mix it with a spoon."

"I don't even see a spoon. Just some knives."

"Jesus. I have a plastic spoon here. The curly-haired lady gave it to me. But you can't boil it, the plastic would melt. That's the problem with plastic."

She lifted the baby out of the bassinet and put him onto the bed. The baby had long black curls. He was wrapped in a flowered towel. He stretched out.

Two feet wrapped in enormous blue booties emerged from the towel.

"You're also cursed when it comes to chairs," said Osvaldo. He went out onto the balcony and found a folding chair with a ripped fabric seat. He carried it inside and sat down.

"I'm cursed when it comes to everything," she said, sitting on the bed and slipping her shirt off to nurse.

"But you're supposed to weigh him first. You haven't weighed the baby," he said.

"How can I weigh him without a scale? I just have to estimate."

"Do you want me to run down to the pharmacy and rent you a scale?"

"Are you willing to pay for the rental?"

"Yes, I am."

"I thought you were a cheapskate. You always told me you were poor and a cheapskate. You always say that you don't own anything—even the bed you sleep in at night belongs to your wife."

"That's true. I'm poor and a cheapskate. But I'm willing to pay the rent for your baby scale."

"Go later. Afterwards. For the moment, don't move from that chair. I like having company while I mix the milk. I worry I'll make a mistake. Or that it'll come out lumpy. At the boardinghouse I had the curly-haired lady. I would call her and she'd come right over. Except at night. She never came at night."

"I can't stay here forever," he said. "I have to go see my wife later."

"You're separated. Why would you go see your wife?"

"I spend time with my daughter. And I see her too. I visit them almost every day."

"Why did you split up?"

"Because we're too different to live together."

"Different how?"

"Just different. She's rich. I'm poor. She's very active. I'm lazy. She's crazy about interior design."

"You're not crazy about interior design?"

"Not crazy."

"When you first married were you hoping that you'd just become richer and less lazy?"

"Yes. I made some effort to be less lazy. But it was torture for her. Even when she lay down to sleep, she couldn't stop thinking about her projects. It was like sleeping next to a boiling kettle."

"What types of projects?"

"Oh she always had some project going on. Houses to restore. An old aunt who needed fixing. Wardrobes to paint. Garages to turn into art galleries. Dogs to breed. Quilts to dye."

"And how did you try to become less lazy and more rich?"

"In the beginning I tried doing some things to get richer. But I didn't put anything into it and nothing ever worked out. She didn't care if I earned money. She wanted me to write books. She wanted that. She said so. She was waiting. That was the horrendous part."

"Couldn't you just tell her that you didn't have any books to write."

"I wasn't sure—I might have had a book in me. Sometimes I thought I might have written a book even if that wasn't something she wanted me to do. But she was always on me, waiting, stubborn, pushing. She was intense. I could feel her anticipation on me even when I slept. It was killing me."

"And so you left."

"It all happened in the most extraordinarily calm way. One day I simply told her that I wanted to live alone again. She wasn't shocked. It seemed as if, with time, her ambition for me had wilted. Nothing had really changed except she got these two little lines at the corners of her mouth."

"What about the shop. Does that belong to your wife too?"

"No, that belongs to my uncle who moved to Varese. I've been running it for so many years that it feels like it's mine."

"And you still haven't written any books even though you live alone now. It seems obvious that you can only sell the books that other people write."

"No, I haven't written any books. That's true. How do you know?"

"Michele told me. He said that you're lazy and you never write anything."

"That's true."

"I'd like your wife to come decorate this apartment."

"My wife?"

"Your wife, yes. If she can transform a garage, she can transform this place."

"My wife … My wife would come right over. She'd bring carpenters and electricians. She'd change everything—your whole life. She'd put the baby in daycare and send you to school to learn English. You'd never have a moment's peace. She'd get rid of all your clothes. She'd throw that dragon kimono right into the garbage."

"But it's so cute," she said.

"It's not her style, a kimono with dragons on it. Not Ada's style."

"The curly-haired lady said that I might be able to go with them to Trapani. Her husband is from there and he wants to open a restaurant. If it goes well, he can hire me. They'll need someone to look after the books."

"You know bookkeeping?"

"Everyone knows bookkeeping."

"Except for you, maybe."

"But the curly-haired lady thinks I do. They could give me a room in the apartment above the restaurant. I could do the books, some housekeeping, even look after their baby and mine at the same time. It's located near the train station. With a location like that you can make a mint."

"Have you ever been to Trapani?"

"Never. The curly-haired lady is a little nervous actually. She doesn't know if she'll like Trapani. And she doesn't know if the restaurant will take off. Her husband already has two failed restaurants. It's her money after all. She even took her husband to a psychic. The psychic told her they should stay far away from Southern cities."

"And so?"

"So nothing. She had a nervous breakdown. She thinks it would be a great comfort to have me nearby. If I can't find anything else, I'll go there."

"I'd advise against it."

"What would you advise instead?"

"I wouldn't advise anything. I never give advice."

"Are you going to see Michele tonight?"

"I don't know. Are you looking for advice from Michele?"

"No. But I want him to come see me. I haven't seen him for such a long time. I went to visit him in his studio when I still had a belly. It was toward the end of the pregnancy. I told him I wanted to take a shower, but he told me there wasn't any hot water and he thought the cold water wouldn't be good for me."

"You're cursed when it comes to showers."

"There's nothing I'm not cursed with. I called him when the baby was born. He told me he'd come but he didn't. I wrote his mother too, a few days ago."

"You wrote to his mother? What were you thinking?"

"I just did. I know her. I met her once. I gave the address at the boardinghouse. That was when I thought I'd stay there. I changed my mind. I told the curly-haired lady to forward my letters to your shop. I didn't want her to have this address, in case she tried to come live here. I told the curly-haired lady a few lies. I told her I was going to live in a wonderful apartment with terra-cotta tiles in some rooms and parquet in others. I told her I was going to live with my brother, the antiques dealer. I made you into an antiques dealer. Instead you just sell old books."

"More to the point, you made me into your brother."

"Yes. But in fact I do have a brother. Though he's younger

than me. He's eleven. His name is Paolo. He lives with those relatives I mentioned. I named the baby Paolo Michele. You know I could report Michele to the police. I'm a minor. If I went to court, he'd have to marry me."

"Do you want to marry Michele?"

"No. That would be like marrying my little brother."

"So why would you want to turn him in?"

"I don't want to turn him in. I wouldn't dream of it. I'm just saying that I could if I wanted to. Go see if the water is boiling."

"It's been boiling for a while," he said.

"Turn it off."

"You're not a minor," he said. "You're twenty-two years old. I saw it on your ID."

"That's true. I turned twenty-two in March. But how did you see my ID?"

"You showed me. You wanted me to see the ugly photograph."

"That's true. I remember that now. I tell a lot of lies."

"It seems to me that you tell a lot of useless lies."

"They're not always useless. Sometimes there's a reason. When I told the curly-haired lady there were parquet floors here, I wanted her to be jealous of me. I was tired of asking her for things. A person gets tired of always bothering people. Sometimes you're just feeling down and the only way to cheer yourself up is to talk bull."

"You said that you didn't know if the baby was Michele's."

"I don't know. I'm not a hundred percent sure. I suspect it's his but I slept with a lot of men during that time. I don't know what was going on with me. When I found out I was pregnant I thought I wanted the baby. I was sure I wanted it. I'd never been so sure of anything. I wrote my sister in Genova and she sent me money for an abortion. I wrote her back and told her I was going to keep the money because I didn't want an abortion. She told me I was crazy."

"Can't you ask your sister to come here? Don't you have anyone who can come help?"

"No. That sister is married now to an agriculturist. I wrote her after the baby was born and he answered—this agriculturist I've never even met. He told me they were moving to Germany and that I should go to hell. Not in those exact words but almost."

"I see."

"When a woman's had a baby she wants to show everyone. That's why I want Michele to see him. We're good friends. We had a good time together. He can be so funny. I went out with other men but always had fun with him. It never even crossed my mind to marry him. I'm not even in love with him! I was only in love once, back in Novi Ligure, with my cousin's husband. But we never had sex because my cousin was always around."

"Michele says that he'll get you money. He'll ask his parents. He'll come by too. One way or the other. Though he says that newborns make him nervous."

"I want money. I know he told you to be nice to me but I think you'd be nice anyway, even if he hadn't asked you to. You have a gentle nature. It's weird that you and me never had sex. It's never crossed my mind. Yours either, I bet. Sometimes I wonder if you're gay, but I don't think so."

"No," he said.

"So it never occurs to you to have sex with me?"

"Never."

"Do you think I'm ugly?"

"No."

"Pretty?"

"Pretty."

"But you're not attracted to me. You're indifferent."

"Well, to tell you the truth, yes."

"Go to hell. That's not a very nice thing to say."

"The baby's stopped nursing. He's asleep," said Osvaldo.

"Yes, well this baby is quite a handful."

"He's hardly a handful. He doesn't do anything but sleep."

"He's a handful even when he's sleeping. I know I made a mess of things. Don't think I don't know."

"What's wrong? Are you crying now?"

"Go beat the milk."

"I've never beaten milk in my life," said Osvaldo.

"That doesn't matter. Read the instructions on the box. Jesus Christ. Help me out."

3

December 2, 1970

Dear Michele,

Osvaldo came over last night to tell me you left for London. I'm speechless and very upset. Osvaldo said that you stopped by your father's house to say goodbye but he was sleeping. What does that mean, "you stopped by"? Don't you understand how sick your father is? Povo—or Covo—says that he'll have to be moved to the hospital today.

You asked for shirts and woolens. Osvaldo says you're thinking about spending the whole winter there. You could have called me. You could have gotten me at the phone booth the way you have in the past. I am going to go mad if they don't install a telephone here. I would have come to the airport. I would have brought you clothes. Osvaldo says you left wearing some canvas pants and a red shirt. He says you had nothing, or practically nothing, to change into. You left all your clothes, clean and dirty, at the workshop. He couldn't even remember at first if you had a jacket with you. Then he remembered you did. That was comforting.

He said you showed up at his house early in the morning. And, according to him, this idea of yours to go study sculpture in London was something you'd been contemplating for a

25

while. Because you're sick of painting those owls. I understand that. I'm writing you at this address Osvaldo gave me even though he says it's temporary. The fact that Osvaldo knows this elderly lady who's giving you a room reassures me a little, a very little. It's not as if I haven't figured out that you're running away. I'm not a fool. I'm pleading with you to please answer right away. Explain what you're running away from, or who. Osvaldo was not very helpful on this point. Either he didn't want to tell me or he didn't know.

Either way, you're gone now. I paid Osvaldo back the money you borrowed. Which is to say I paid his wife back. I wrote the check out to his wife. Osvaldo says that his wife always has cash on hand at the house, otherwise there wouldn't have been a way for you to leave on a Saturday. Osvaldo got here last night at ten. He was exhausted from the whole business at the police station, getting your passport renewed, then driving you to the airport, and then he had to go somewhere on the outskirts of the city to pick up his wife's car, which you loaned to someone … Who knows who. He hadn't eaten and I didn't have anything in the house except for some random cheeses Matilde had bought at the supermarket that morning. I put out all the cheese and Matilde made a scene. Matilde then provided the entertainment by talking about French Impressionism. She fanned her face, smoked her pipe, and paced back and forth with her hands in her pockets. I could have killed her. I wanted her to leave so I could ask Osvaldo more about you. The twins were there too playing ping-pong. At last everyone went to sleep.

I asked him if you left because of that Mara Castorelli who wrote me about her baby. Osvaldo told me the baby isn't yours. According to him the girl has nothing to do with your departure. He says she's just a lost soul with no money. There are no chairs in her apartment, or blankets, and he was thinking of bringing her a blanket and chairs from your studio, since they're not doing anyone any good there. He also asked if he could take that green, wood-burning stove, the one with the decoration, by which he means the German stove. I told him that it needs to be disconnected from the exhaust pipe in the wall and it might be too complicated. It made me think of the day I went to buy it for you so I'm sentimental about it. You will certainly say that it's stupid for a person to love a wood stove. Osvaldo told me you never light it because you can never remember to order wood, so you use the electric one instead. I ended up telling him that he could do whatever he wanted with the chairs and the stove. I asked him if you'd gotten involved with any radical political groups. I have this terrible fear that you're going to end up joining the Tupamaros. He said he didn't know who you'd been associating with recently. He said it was possible that you were running from something. He wasn't very clear.

I can't figure out if I like him. He's polite. It's the kind of politeness that makes you feel full, as if you've eaten too much jam. He has that red face and he's always laughing. But I don't know what there is to laugh about. Sometimes I look at him and wonder if he isn't a pedophile. I could never really understand why you were such good friends. You're a child and he's a grown man of thirty-six, maybe thirty-eight years old. You'll just say that I worry too much about you. There is an endless list of things I can worry about.

He says he doesn't have any relatives who work at the phone company but his wife Ada might know someone. He promised he'd ask her for me. I don't know how any of us would survive without Ada. She gave you cash to leave. She called someone about your passport, which you wouldn't have gotten otherwise. You should write and thank her. Osvaldo says that she was already up at seven to treat her terra-cotta pavement with petroleum. I have terra-cotta tiles too but we've never treated them with petroleum. In fact, they are so dark I don't think Cloti washes them at all.

The morning of the day before yesterday, Matilde came with me to visit your father. He was sitting up in bed when we got there, smoking and making phone calls and for a few minutes he didn't seem sick at all. He was on the phone with an architect. I don't know if you're aware that the week before he fell ill your father bought a tower on the Isola del Giglio. He didn't pay much for it, at least that's what he claims. As far as I can tell it's a crumbling tower, probably full of weeds and snakes. Your father got it into his head that he'd add bathrooms and walls, and so on. He wouldn't get off the phone when we walked in, he just waved at Matilde and kept talking with that gravelly voice. She acted patient and started leafing through a magazine. When your father hung up the phone he told her that she seemed much fatter. Then she started in on him about the time she'd given him a draft of her novel, *Polenta and Poison*, to read but that he'd left it in the bar at the train station in Florence. It was the only clean, typed copy and it was in a blue folder. Matilde wrote to the bar but the blue folder was never found. After that she lost all desire to retype and revise it, she was so discouraged and disappointed. The fact that he'd lost the blue folder seemed central to the problem. Then they started arguing about the vineyard near Spoleto that they own together. She wants to sell it and your father doesn't. The other morning your father had mentioned he was sorry he'd lost the blue folder but that *Polenta and Poison* was an inane novel and the world was better without it. Then he had a wave of pain, nausea and pain. Then the architect walked in—the one who's working on the tower—but your father didn't have any desire to look at tiles and pick little blue flowers or little brown flowers. The architect is six feet six inches tall. He seems more like an idea. There was something completely incompetent about him. We told him to come back later and he threw the tiles into his bag, grabbed his trench coat, and ran off.

I need you to write immediately with an address that's not temporary. I'm thinking I can send you some money and clothes with someone who is headed to London. I'll find someone. In the meantime, I'll keep writing you at this address. I'll send news about your father. I think I'll tell him you had to rush off because they were closing registration at the sculpture school. Either way he considers you to be very responsible. He thinks that you do everything the only way it should be done.

My rabbits arrived. There are four of them. I called in a carpenter to build cages. I knew I wouldn't be able to rely on you for this tiny favor. I understand it's not your fault. But the way things go it seems like I can never count on any little favors from you.

Your mother

4

December 3, 1970—London

Dear Angelica,

I left in such a hurry because they called in the middle of the night to tell me Anselmo had been arrested. I called you from the airport but you didn't answer.

I'm sending this letter with someone—he'll bring it to you by hand. His name is Ray. I met him here. He's from Ostend. He can be trusted. Give him somewhere to sleep if you have room. He needs to stay in Rome for a few days.

I need you to go to my house right away. Make up some excuse to get the keys from Osvaldo. Tell him you need a book. Tell him whatever you want. Don't forget to bring a suitcase or bag with you. There's a dismantled machine gun wrapped in a towel, inside the wood stove. I totally forgot about it before I left. That will seem strange to you but it's how it was. My friend Oliviero brought it to me one night a few weekends ago because he thought the police might search his place. I told him to tuck it in the stove. I never light that stove. It burns wood and I never have wood. I hid the gun in the stove and then forgot all about it. I remembered after I was on the plane, already in the air. It was like I suddenly got drenched in a boiling sweat. They say fear makes you break out in a cold sweat. That's not true. Sweat can be boiling. I had to take off my sweater. You should bring a suitcase or bag to put the gun into. Unload it onto someone you'd never suspect. Like the woman who comes to clean for you. Or you could get it back to Oliviero. His name is Oliviero Marzullo. I don't have his address but someone does. Now that I think about it, the gun is so old and rusty you could just throw it in the Tiber. I'm not asking Osvaldo to do this for me, I'm asking you. I'd actually prefer if Osvaldo never knew. I don't want him to think I'm a complete imbecile. But if you feel strongly that you want to tell Osvaldo, go ahead. If he ends up thinking I'm an idiot, what do I care.

Of course my passport had expired. Of course Osvaldo helped me get it renewed, all in a matter of hours. Gianni was at the airport too and we got into it because Gianni thinks there's a fascist spy in the group. Maybe more than one. I'm sure he's just imagining things. Gianni won't leave Rome but he never spends more than one night in the same place.

I stopped by to see our father before I left. Osvaldo waited for me in the car. Father was fast asleep. He looked very old and very sick.

I'm well. My room here is long and narrow and the wallpaper is tattered. Everything about this place is long and narrow. There's a hallway and all the bedrooms open off the hallway. There are five of us boarding here. We pay four pounds a week. The landlady is a Romanian Jew who sells skin cream.

When you have time, will you go see a girl I know who is staying on Via dei Prefetti. I don't remember the address but Osvaldo has it. Her name is Mara Castorelli. She just had a baby. I gave her money for an abortion but she didn't get it. I

slept with her a few times so the baby could be mine. She was
with a lot of men though. Bring her a little money if you can.

Michele

Angelica was sprawled on the couch in her dining room reading the letter. It was a small, very dark, dining room. The table
took up almost all the space and was overflowing with books
and papers. A lamp and a typewriter teetered on top of the
stacks. Oreste, her husband, worked at the table, but he was
in the bedroom now sleeping because he worked nights at the
newspaper and usually slept until four in the afternoon. The
kitchen door was open and she could see her friend Sonia with
her daughter Flora, sitting with the boy who'd brought the letter. Flora was eating bread dunked in Ovaltine. She looked like
a green, five-year-old girl lizard—wearing a blue pinafore and
red wool tights. Angelica's friend Sonia was hunched over the
sink washing last night's dishes. She was tall, shy, and wore
glasses. Her long, black hair was pulled back into a ponytail.
The boy who'd brought the letter was eating a plate of reheated
penne with tomato sauce leftover from Oreste's dinner. He
wore a faded turquoise windbreaker that he didn't want to take
off because he'd caught a chill while traveling. His short, chest-
nut beard was sparse and well groomed.

Angelica finished reading the letter and stood up from the
couch to look for her shoes under the carpet. Her tights were
the color of moss. She was wearing a rumpled sweater that
she'd been wearing since the day before at the hospital. Her
father had gone into surgery and died overnight.

Angelica twisted her fine blonde hair into a bun on top of
her head and secured it in place with several combs. She was
twenty-three years old. She was pale, tall, and her face was a

little too long. Her eyes were green like her mother's but shaped differently—long, narrow, and slanted. She pulled a flowered black tote down from the wardrobe. She already had Michele's studio keys from Osvaldo because she had planned to collect his dirty laundry and take it to the cleaners. The keys were in her jacket pocket. It was a black nylon jacket she'd bought used at Porta Portese. She put it on, called into the kitchen that she was going out shopping, and left.

Her Fiat was parked in front of Chiesa Nuova. She climbed into the car and sat for a moment without moving. Then she drove toward Piazza Farnese. She remembered a day last October when she'd run into her father on Via dei Giubbonari. He was walking toward her with his long stride, hands in his pockets, long black curls swept back in the wind, his tie blowing, that black alpaca coat, as always, rumpled and unbuttoned, his broad brown face and large mouth, the expression bitter and disgusted, as always. She had been coming out of the movies with her daughter. He extended his hand, soft, sweaty, limp. They hadn't kissed each other in years. They didn't have much to say either since they didn't see each other often. They got some coffee and stood at the bar. He bought the child a big, cream pastry. When Angelica expressed doubt that it was fresh, he was offended and said that he always came to this bar and he'd never had an old pastry. He told her that a friend of his lived right upstairs, an Irish cello player. While they were drinking their coffee, the Irish woman showed up. She was plump and not beautiful, her nose looked like a shoe. They were going out to look for coats because the Irish woman wanted to buy one. They all went together to a clothing store in Piazza del Paradiso. The Irish woman tried on coats. Her father bought a poncho with pictures of deer on it for Flora.

The Irish woman picked out a long black buckskin coat lined with white fur that she was very pleased with. Her father paid, pulling a handful of crumpled bills from his pocket. The edge of a handkerchief stuck out of his pocket. He always had a bit of handkerchief coming out of his pocket. Then they went to the Medusa Gallery where her father was hanging a show that was about to open. The gallery owners were two young men in leather jackets who were determined to handwrite the invitations to the opening. The paintings were almost all hung and there was a big portrait of her mother, painted many years earlier when her mother and father were still together. Her mother was at the window, hands folded under her chin. She was wearing a blue and white striped shirt, her hair a cloud of fiery red. Her face was a parched triangle, sardonic and full of lines, while her eyes were heavy, contemptuous, and dim. Angelica remembered their house on Pieve di Cadore where they lived when he'd painted that picture. She recognized the window and the green awning over the terrace. The house had been sold later. Her father paused in front of the painting, his hands in his pockets, and he spent a long time praising the palette which he described as acid and cruel. Then he commenced praising every one of his paintings. Recently he'd started working on an enormous scale, using canvases upon which he'd piled every manner of object. He'd discovered a heaping technique. Boats, cars, bicycles, trucks, dolls, soldiers, gravestones, naked women, and dead animals, floating in a murky green haze. In his bitter, gravelly voice, her father said that no one working in that moment was able to paint with such vastness and precision. His work was tragic and solemn, gigantic and detailed. He referred to "my pain-ting," landing on the t with an asthmatic flourish—solitary and painful. Angelica didn't

34

believe a word of what he was saying and thought that the Irish woman and the gallery owners didn't either—maybe her father didn't believe a word he was saying or the grating way he was saying it. His voice echoed piercing and isolated. A broken record. Angelica suddenly remembered a song her father used to sing while he was painting, a childhood memory. It had been many years since she'd been there when he was painting.

> Non avemo ni canones
> Ni tanks ni aviones
> Ay Carmelà!

She asked him if he still sang *Ay Carmelà!* when he painted and he seemed surprisingly moved. He said that no, he didn't sing anymore, the new paintings took too much effort. He painted while balancing on a ladder, and he sweated so much he had to change his shirt every two hours. He seemed suddenly anxious to be liberated from the Irish woman. He told her that it was getting dark and that she should go home. He wasn't able to walk her because he had a dinner engagement. The Irish woman hailed a taxi. He spoke sharply to her about always taking too many taxis even though she came from the remote Irish countryside where there were no taxis, just fog, peat, and sheep. He took Angelica under the arm and walked her and the child home to Via dei Banchi Vecchi. On the way there, he started complaining. He was alone. His butler was a fool who used to work in a car repair shop. No one ever visited him. He practically never saw the twins who'd gotten fat recently, they were only fourteen years old and weighed fifty-eight kilos each. One hundred and sixteen kilos all together, he said, it was too much. He almost never saw Viola, who, to make matters worse, he could barely stand because she had no sense of irony. She and her husband were shacked up in his parents' house. So many people under one roof—in-laws, uncles, aunts, grandchildren. It was a commune. All those relatively insignificant people. Pharmacists! Not that he had a problem with pharmacies, he'd said, ducking into a drugstore to buy some Alka-Seltzer for the great pain he had "right here" he said, pointing to the middle of his chest, a dull pain, maybe that old ulcer—his aged and faithful life companion. He'd barely seen Michele recently, which troubled him. He'd agreed it was the right thing when Michele moved out to live on his own, but it was sad. When he spoke of Michele his voice softened, as if beaten—it didn't have that grating quality. But Michele was always with that Osvaldo man now. He couldn't quite understand what kind of person Osvaldo was. Obviously he was very nice. Polite. Unobtrusive. Michele dragged him around everywhere, even to Via San Sabastianello when he came over to do his laundry. Likely he needed Osvaldo to give him a lift in the car. Michele didn't have a car anymore. He'd lost his license after hitting that old nun. She died but it wasn't Michele's fault. Not entirely Michele's fault. He had only just learned how to drive and was speeding because he was going to his mother's who needed him because she was depressed. She was always depressed. Their mother, he said, lowering his voice to a husky whisper, couldn't stand to be alone and in her infinite stupidity hadn't known that Cavalieri had been planning for some time to leave her. She was naive. At forty-four years old, she had the mentality of a teenage girl. Forty-two, said Angelica, she's turning forty-three soon. Her father made a brisk calculation on his fingers. She is more naive than the twins, he said. And worse, the twins aren't disingenuous. They're cool and calculating—like two wolves. Either way Cavaliere had never impressed him much. He never, never ever seemed nice. His sloped shoulders and long white fingers, his hair in ringlets. From the side he looked like a hawk. Her father said he could always recognize a hawk. When they reached Angelica's front door, he said he didn't feel like coming up because he didn't care much for her husband Oreste—he's pedantic. Sanctimonious. Her father didn't kiss Angelica or the little girl, but he chucked the girl under her chin and squeezed Angelica's arm. He encouraged her to come to the opening the next day. The show was going to be a "big deal." He left. Angelica missed the opening because she went to a conference in Naples with her husband. After that day, she only saw her father again two or three times. He was sick in bed and her mother was there. He didn't say anything to her. One time he was on the phone. Another time he was feeling unwell and just gestured in her direction, distracted and disgusted.

Angelica climbed six flights up to the studio. She turned on the light as she entered. There was a bed in the middle of the room, the sheets and blankets in disarray. Angelica recognized her mother's beautiful blankets. Mother loved buying nice blankets, warm and lightweight, soft with velvet trim, lovely pale colors. The floor was cluttered with empty bottles, newspapers, and paintings. She glanced at the paintings—vultures, owls, abandoned houses. The dirty laundry was by the window, along with a pair of wadded up jeans, a tea kettle, an ashtray full of cigarette butts, and a plate of oranges. The wood stove was in the center of the room. It was large and round, with a green enamel door in a delicate ornamental design that looked like lace. Angelica reached an arm into the stove and fished out a bundle wrapped in an old frayed towel. She tossed it into the tote bag. She also took the laundry and the oranges. She left the workshop and walked for a while in the damp, foggy morning, turning up her jacket collar to shield her mouth. She dropped off the dirty clothes at a nearby laundromat, called Fast Wash. She had to wait at the counter while they counted the clothes one by one. Then she got back in her car. She drove slowly through traffic to the Lungotevere Ripa. She climbed down the stairs leading to the river bank. She threw the bundle into the river. A child asked her what she'd thrown into the river. She told him they were rotten oranges.

"Non avemo ni canones … ni tanks ni aviones" she sang as she made her way home through the traffic. All at once she realized her face was wet with tears. She laughed, sobbed, and wiped her tears away with her jacket sleeve. When she got close to her house, she bought some pork loin to poach with potatoes. She also bought two bottles of beer and a box of sugar. Then she bought a black scarf and a pair of black stockings to wear to her father's funeral.

5

December 8, 1970—London

Dear Mamma,

After some moments of indecision and for reasons not easily explained in a letter, I've decided not to return to Rome. When Osvaldo called to tell me that Papa had died, I went to find out about flights, but then I didn't leave. I know you told everyone that I had pneumonia.

Thank you for the clothes and money. The person who brought them, Signora Peroni's nephew, couldn't give me any news about you because he'd never met you but he brought news of Osvaldo and gave me back my watch that I'd given to Osvaldo to hold while I rushed to shower and then forgot to get back from him at the airport. Thank him for me. I don't have time to write to him directly.

I'm leaving London for Sussex. I can stay with a linguistics professor there. I'll have to do dishes, light the stove, and walk the dogs. For the time being I've given up on sculpture school. I prefer dogs and dishes.

I'm sorry I didn't get to build cages for your rabbits. But I'll do it when I get back. Kisses to you and my sisters.

Michele

6

December 8, 1970

Dear Michele,

Regarding the little thing you forgot in your stove, mission accomplished. I threw it into the Tiber—it was, as you said, all rusty.

I have not yet gone to see the girl on Via dei Prefetti. I haven't had time. The baby has a cold. And you said I should bring her money, but I don't have any at the moment.

Our father was buried three days ago. I will write again as soon as I can.

Angelica

7

December 12, 1970

Dear Michele,

I just received your short letter. I have no idea what kept you from coming back for your father's funeral. I can't conceive of anything that would keep a person from coming home when there's a death in the family. I don't understand. I have to wonder if you'll come when I die. Yes, we told a number of family members that you were in London yesterday, sick with pneumonia.

I'm pleased you're going to Sussex. The air there must be very good and it makes me happy when any of you are in the countryside. Taking you on country excursions when you were little bored me to death. I thought that every extra day spent in the outdoors was good for you children. After you moved in with your father, you'd spend the entire summer in Rome, and that drove me crazy. He didn't like the countryside. He loved the sea. He'd send you and the maid out every morning to Ostia and said that was good enough.

You didn't say whether you were also going to be cooking for this professor of linguistics. Write me if you have to cook too, and I'll send some recipes. Matilde finds recipes in newspapers and magazines and pastes them all in a giant notebook.

Send me your phone number in Sussex, even though I'll still have to call you from a pay phone because they haven't put in my line yet. The pay phone is in a tavern that's always full of people, and I'm worried I might cry if we talk. It's not the sort of place for phone calls and crying.

Your father's death hit me very hard. I feel much more alone now. He didn't support me because he didn't care about me. Or your sisters. You were the only person he cared about. His affection for you didn't have anything to do with you, it was an invention, something he imagined you to be. I don't know how to explain why I feel more alone now. Maybe it was because we shared memories. Memories only he and I knew, even though we never spoke of them when we met. I realize now it didn't matter that we didn't talk about them. They were a presence in the hours we spent together at Cafe Canova, those oppressive, never-ending hours. They weren't happy memories because your father and I were never happy together. Even if we had been briefly and occasionally happy, everything got sullied, ripped up, and destroyed. But people don't love each other only for happy memories. At a certain point in life, you realize that you just love the memories.

It might seem strange to you that I can't go into Cafe Canova anymore. If I went there I would start sobbing like an idiot and I'm sure of one thing, I don't want to cry in front of people.

We had to fire your father's butler, the one whose name I can't remember, Federico or Enrico, and Ada took him on. Matilde was convinced that I should have hired him but I didn't want to because he seems like a fool. Osvaldo says that Ada will teach him everything because apparently she's a kind of genius in training butlers to become impeccable and inscrutable. I don't know how she will make this insipid, bewildered boy impeccable, he makes me think of a boar. But Osvaldo claims that Ada's art has no limit when it comes to molding domestics.

Matilde and I have been going every day to Via San Sebastianello to sort through your father's papers and make an inventory of his paintings before we put them in storage. I don't know what to do about the furniture because neither Viola nor Angelica have room in their houses for it. It's all big furniture and takes up a lot of space. We were thinking of selling it. Osvaldo and your father's cousin, Lillino, came over yesterday to look at the paintings. Lillino is leaving today for Mantua and I'm delighted because I can't stand him. Lillino has recommended hanging onto the paintings for now because there's not much of a market for your father's work. His most recent pieces are enormous, and to tell you the truth I think they're dreadful. I can tell that even Osvaldo thinks they're awful. I can tell even if he hasn't said a word. But Lillino says they are magnificent and that the world will discover them one day and they'll be worth a fortune. Matilde just tosses her head and purses her lips, and then expresses the utmost admiration. I get dizzy when I look at them. Why in the world did he start doing those huge, shocking paintings. I did take that old portrait of me from years ago sitting at the window of the house in Pieve di Cadore. Your father sold the house just a few months after. The painting is hanging in the living room now and I'm looking at it while writing you. Of all your father's paintings, it's the one most dear to me. We separated very soon after that period, the end of that summer after we got back to Rome. We were living on Corso Trieste then. You and Viola and Angelica were staying at Chianciano with Aunt Cecilia. Maybe your sisters knew what was going on but you didn't because you were little, only six years old. I left the house on Corso Trieste one morning and never went back. I took the twins and went to my parents who were on vacation in Roccadimezzo. I got to Roccadimezzo after a train trip that I can't even remember to describe because the twins were throwing up the entire time. My parents were there, staying in a good hotel, happy, eating well, talking walks in the fields. They weren't expecting me at all, because I hadn't warned them. It was late when I got to the hotel with three suitcases and the twins soaked in vomit. My parents were stunned when they saw me. I hadn't slept in a week because of all the anguish and indecision and my face must have been a wreck. My mother had her first heart attack two months later. I've always thought that mother's heart attack was caused by seeing me arrive in Roccodimezzo in the middle of the night in that state. She had a second heart attack that spring and died.

Your father decided you would live with him. You would go with him and the girls would stay with me. He bought the place on Via San Sebastianello and moved you all in. There was that old cook who stayed on for just a few months, I can't remember her name. Maybe you remember her. For the longest time I couldn't set foot in that house because he wouldn't see me. I called you and you cried over the phone. What a horrendous memory. I waited with the twins for you at Villa Borghese and that old cook wearing a monkey-fur coat would meet us there. In the early days you would scream and throw yourself to the ground when the old cook said it was time to go home, but eventually there would be a transformation and your face would grow hard and calm and you'd climb onto your scooter and leave. I can still see you moving away, upright in your little coat, in such a hurry. I had so much hatred built up toward your

44

father, I had it in me to take a gun over to San Sebastianello and shoot him. A mother probably shouldn't tell her son such things. It's not instructive. But the question is, how does anyone know what instructive is, and if there's even such a thing as an upbringing. I didn't bring you up. I wasn't there. How could I teach you. I just got to see you in the afternoon sometimes at Via Borghese. Your father certainly didn't teach you anything, having gotten it into his head that you were born knowing everything. No one brought you up. And you turned out pretty oblivious. Though I'm not sure you would have been less oblivious if you'd had a better upbringing. Your sisters are maybe less oblivious than you are but they're peculiar too, and oblivious, one of them in one respect and the other in another. I didn't teach them anything. Or maybe I taught them something but it was the wrong thing, because sometimes I feel like a person I don't like very much. In order to teach another person you have to have some modicum of faith in yourself, and compassion too.

I don't remember when or how your father and I stopped hating each other. He slapped me once in the lawyer's office. He hit me so hard my nose bled. Lillino was there, along with the lawyer, and they had me lie on the couch while Lillino went down to the pharmacy to get me an iron supplement. Your father locked himself in the bathroom and wouldn't come out. He gets scared around blood and felt sick. I see now that I wrote "he gets scared" in the present tense. I can't seem to remember your father is dead. Lillino and the lawyer were banging and rattling on the bathroom door. He was very pale when he came out and his hair was matted because he'd put his head under the faucet. It makes me laugh to think about that scene now. There were so many times I wanted to talk about it with your father, to laugh with him, but our relationship fossilized. We were never able to laugh together again. I think after he slapped me he was able to stop hating me. He never wanted me to come to Via San Sebastianello but sometimes he came to Villa Borghese himself instead of sending the cook. I stopped hating him. One time at Villa Borghese we were playing Blind Fly with you on the grass and I tripped and fell and he cleaned the mud off my dress with his handkerchief. He was on his knees cleaning off the mud, I looked down at his long, black curls and I could tell that there wasn't even a shadow of hatred between us anymore. That was a happy moment. Happiness made out of nothing, because I knew that even if my relationship with your father wasn't about hatred anymore it was still made of something sad and cowardly. But I remember the sunset, beautiful pink clouds over the city, and for the first time in a long time I was almost serene, almost happy.

I have nothing to tell you about your father's death. Matilde and I were at the hospital the day before he died. He and Matilde chatted and then fought. He called the architect to talk about the tower. He said that he'd bought the tower primarily for you because of your great passion for the sea and that now you'd be able to spend whole summers there. You can invite all your friends because there are a ton of rooms. I know you don't have any passion for the sea, you're as likely to sit on the shore, fully dressed and drenched with sweat in the middle of August. But I didn't want to contradict him so I didn't say a word. And he kept on fantasizing about the tower. He seemed to think buying it was a stroke of genius and a great bargain, he said it was a shame I never had strokes of genius because of the house I bought, which must have been a huge mistake, tacky and expensive. I didn't answer him. Then a group of his friends arrived down at reception but he said he was tired and didn't want any guests. Biagioni, Casalis, Maschera, and an Irish girl I think he was dating. I sent Matilde down to talk to them. That gave me and him some time alone. He told me that I was welcome to spend the summer in the tower. But he didn't want the twins to come because of their transistor radios, he wouldn't get any rest in the afternoon. I told him he was being unfair to the twins. If you were to show up at the tower with a whole group of friends he wouldn't be able to take an afternoon nap either. So he said that maybe the twins could come once in a while too. But not Viola and Angelica. Viola could go to the countryside with her in-laws, it was ugly, there were flies everywhere, but she had fun there. Angelica with her boring husband. Did she love him? Maybe she did love him. Either way, he didn't want Oreste in his tower because there was that time Oreste said something critical about Cézanne. The imbecile. How can a frog form opinions about Cézanne. He said he was going to exercise the utmost attention and discretion about who to invite every summer. Every summer? Actually, no, all the time, because he was planning on living in the tower year-round. For example, he never wanted Matilde to come to the tower. He'd never liked her, even when they were children. He had no idea why I'd taken her in. I told him that I was lonely and needed company. I preferred Matilde to no one at all. And I feel sorry for Matilde because she doesn't have a cent to her name. She could always sell the vineyard, your father said. I reminded him that they'd already sold the vineyard quite a while ago. They'd sold it off little by little and now there was a motel where the vineyard used to be. Then he said that it was unbearable to think of a motel standing where there had once been such a splendid vineyard. He thought it was rather unkind of me to remind him. He turned over and didn't want to talk anymore. He wouldn't even talk to Matilde. Then Matilde told me that the Irish girl had collapsed in tears and Biagioni and Casalis had to carry her off.

Your father's operation was at eight in the morning. We were all there, in the waiting room. Me, Matilde, Angelica, Viola, Elio, and Oreste. The twins were staying at a friend's house. The surgery didn't take long. I later found out that they'd cut him open and then closed him right back up because there was nothing more to be done. Matilde and I were in the room with him when he woke, and Angelica and Viola were in the waiting room. He didn't say anything. He died at two in the morning.

A lot of people came to the funeral. Biagioni spoke first and then Maschera. Lately your father couldn't stand either of them. He said they didn't get his new work. He said they were jealous of him and he called them hawks. He said he could always tell a hawk.

Clearly you don't read my letters or maybe you read them and forget about them immediately. You can't build cages for my rabbits when you get back because I already hired a carpenter to do it. There are four rabbits. Four. But I don't know if I'll stay out here in the country much longer. Maybe I hate it here.

Filippo came to your father's funeral.

Your mother
Ti abbraccio

The letter written and sealed, Adriana put on a camel-hair coat and wrapped a black wool scarf around her head. It was five in the afternoon. She went down to the kitchen. Looked in the refrigerator. She stared hatefully at the ox tongue Matilde was marinating in a salad bowl. She thought that the tongue was probably a bad cut, and it would be around for months. Neither Matilde nor the twins were home. Cloti was in bed with the flu. Adriana checked in on her. Cloti was in her bathrobe under the covers, her head wrapped in a towel. The twins' transistor radio was on the nightstand. Adriana told her to check her temperature. She waited. Bobby Solo was singing on the radio. Cloti said she really liked Bobby Solo. It was the first time that Adriana heard her express an opinion or positive thought. Usually the things Cloti expressed were accompanied by a deep sigh that had to do with her personal troubles, the lumpy mattress, the drafty window. Adriana said she was sorry not to be able to move the television into her room because it was too heavy. Cloti said that there was nothing good on television in the afternoon. Evening is better. She didn't have a television in her room at her other job either, and there, they had provided her with all the comforts. She listed the comforts provided to her at her other job. A lovely big room. Nice white and gold furniture and a rug that was so valuable she worried about having it in her room. A soft mattress. Heating and air conditioning that regulated the temperature throughout the house. The lawyer was always traveling so there was nothing to do there except look after the cat. Adriana pulled the thermometer from Cloti's armpit. Her temperature was normal. Cloti said she was definitely getting a fever because she had chills, hot and cold, and a strange ache in her head. Adriana asked if she wanted some tea. Cloti refused the tea. There was one thing she didn't like about working for the lawyer, she said, and that was when he came home in the evening he wanted her sit with him in the parlor and make conversation. She never knew what to say. Not that the lawyer had propositioned her. He was respectful and understood what she was like from the very start. He just wanted to make conversation. That's why she left. Because she didn't feel like talking. And there had been gossip. The lawyer's sister came to visit and made a comment about a particular osso buco. Another time the sister told Cloti to bathe because she smelled. Cloti washed herself every morning, armpits and feet, so there was no way she smelled. She only took a bath once a month because it made her feel faint afterward. But those were excuses. To be honest there was gossip. But now she understood that it'd been a mistake to leave. A giant mistake.

Adriana went to get the car out of the garage. She opened the gate. She hated the two dwarf spruce trees that Matilde had planted by the gate. Fake alpine in the middle of that bare garden. She hoped they would die. The road ran in tight curves through the fields. The car lurched. It had been a sunny day and there was hardly any snow on the ground. The sun was still hitting the village and the sides of the hill, but dusk with its cold, gray, thin fog was rising over the plain. The twins weren't home yet. She hated Matilde who had gone to buy olives and capers for the boiled ox tongue. There were no houses at all for a long stretch, then there was a low house with a thread of smoke coming out of a vent in the window. Two photographers lived there. The man was outside on the stairs washing dishes in a blue plastic bucket. The woman was wearing a red dress and stockings that had runs in them. She was hanging laundry on the line. For some reason seeing the couple gave her a sharp feeling of desperation, as if they were the only thing the universe had to offer. There was another long muddy stretch, desiccated hedges, fallow fields. Finally she got to the main road, with its constant stream of cars. At the side of the road men in overalls gathered around a dumpster.

She thought of Filippo's wife, who'd come to the funeral.

She was pregnant. She'd worn a yellow jacket with big tortoise shell buttons running over her belly. Her face was angular and young, her hair was smoothly pulled back into a tiny bun. She stayed next to Filippo. Ruddy, serious, hard, purse in her hands. Filippo was the same. He took off his glasses and put them back on. He ran his long fingers through his coarse gray curls. He looked around, on his face an expression of feigned resolution and feigned authority. In order to get to the town center, you had to follow a steep ridge road lit with neon streetlamps. At the moment, the lamp poles were wrapped in paper garlands in preparation for a parade. She mailed the letter in town. She bought eggs from a woman with a grill and basket who was sitting in front of the church. They talked about the wind that had come up suddenly, the black clouds blowing in over the roofs, the rustling paper garlands. She went into a cafe to call Angelica, putting a finger in one ear to block out the noise. She told Angelica to come to lunch on Sunday. They were going to have boiled ox tongue. There was static on the line and Angelica couldn't hear. They said their goodbyes quickly. She got back in the car. The day Filippo had come to tell her he was getting married he'd brought Angelica. He wanted Angelica there in case she fell apart and cried. Foolish of him. Adriana rarely fell apart and cried. She kept everything inside. She was solid like an oak. In any event, she'd been expecting it for some time. But that was when the house on Via dei Villini became odious. After Filippo left, she lay down in the bedroom with the arched ceiling and cried while Angelica held her hand.

8

"SHE SEEMS LIKE a complete idiot," said Ada.

"Not a *complete* idiot," said Osvaldo.

"Completely," said Ada.

"She's not stupid, she's ignorant," said Osvaldo.

"I don't see the difference," said Ada.

"Either way, she can fry eggs," said Osvaldo. "I know Signora Peroni's mother. She has simple tastes."

"This is not about just frying eggs," said Ada. "I know Signora Peroni's mother better than you do and she's not easily satisfied. She keeps an orderly house. The floors waxed and polished. A crying baby is going to get on her nerves."

"I didn't know how else to help her and she's breaking my heart with that baby," said Osvaldo.

"So you decided to dump her on the Peronis," said Ada.

"The Peronis love babies."

"They love babies who are passing by in strollers at Villa Borghese, not babies living in their house and screaming all night long."

Osvaldo had eaten at Ada's house and now they were sitting in the living room. He was gluing stamps into an album for Elisabetta. Ada was knitting. Elisabetta was out on the veranda with a friend playing cards. The girls were sitting on the ground in grave silence.

"There's no point gluing those stamps," said Ada. "It's better for her to do it herself and she enjoys it."

Osvaldo secured the album shut with an elastic band and went over to the window to look out. The glassed-in veranda with its giant potted plants ran the length of the living room. He knocked on the glass but Elisabetta was absorbed in her game and didn't even look up.

"The azalea came out marvelous," he said.

"You know I have a green thumb. That's hardly news. It looked dead when they brought it to me. It's from Michele's father's house. The butler brought it. They were going to throw it out but it occurred to him to bring it here instead."

"You see, he has thoughts."

"Sometimes. Not often. But he's not unkind. I taught him how to serve dinner properly."

Osvaldo was on the verge of saying, see, you have a green thumb for butlers, but it struck him that it was some kind of double entendre so he stopped himself, then blushed anyway.

"That girl of yours, though, will never learn anything," said Ada.

"She doesn't need to serve dinner at the Peronis'. They all just sit in the kitchen together."

"What about the apartment on Via dei Prefetti? What happened to that?"

"Nothing. She goes back on Sundays. She leaves the baby at the Peronis' and goes to Via dei Prefetti. She relaxes. Has a girlfriend over."

"Is she sleeping with anyone?"

"Maybe. I don't know. She says she's tired of sex. All she thinks about is the baby. She's stopped nursing. She gives him bottles."

"In other words, Signora Peroni gives him bottles."

"I think so."

"That baby looks a lot like Michele. I'm sure he's his," said Ada.

"You think?"

"Yes. Identical."

"The baby has black hair. Michele is a redhead."

"Hair doesn't count. It's the facial expressions. His mouth. I think Michele should come back and give that child his name. That's what any decent person would do. Of course, he isn't. He wouldn't have to marry her. You can't marry a girl like that. But give the baby a name, yes. What are you thinking of doing with the studio?"

"I don't know. You tell me. For now, a friend of Michele's from London is staying there, a guy named Ray. But I think he's only staying for a few days."

"It was a huge relief when Michele left. Now you've gone and installed another one in there."

"He didn't have anywhere to go. He was staying with Angelica but her husband wanted him out of the house. They fought about politics. Angelica's husband has ironclad ideas and doesn't like them to be questioned."

"If they were really ironclad he wouldn't mind discussing them. If he gets that angry, it means his ideas are more like cheese than iron. I know Angelica's husband. He's a modest person. A functionary. An apparatchik who comes off like an accountant."

"You're not wrong."

"I'll bet their marriage doesn't last long. Though aren't all marriages short-lived these days? We had a short marriage for that matter."

"It survived exactly four years," said Osvaldo.

"Does that seem long to you? Four years?"

"No, I'm just saying how long it lasted. Exactly four."

"To tell you the truth, I don't think much of these boys you've got hanging around now. They are wild and dangerous. I almost prefer the accountants. As far as the studio itself goes, I don't care either way. I just don't want it to go up in smoke."

"Well. Especially since I'd go up in smoke along with it because I live right upstairs. And the seamstress on the top floor. But this Ray guy doesn't seem like the sort of person who blows things up. I don't think he even knows what gunpowder is."

"Please don't introduce me to Ray. Don't bring him here. You always brought Michele over. I didn't like him. He wasn't pleasant. He'd just sit there and stare at me with those little green eyes. He thought I was stupid. But I just didn't think he was very nice. I paid for him to leave. I helped him, but it wasn't out of sympathy."

"It was niceness," said Osvaldo.

"Yes, that, and because I was thrilled by the idea that I'd never have to see him again. Although I think it's a very big deal that he didn't come back when his father died. A very big deal."

"He was worried about getting arrested," said Osvaldo. "They arrested two or three other people from his group."

"All the same, it's a very big deal. And you agree. You were shocked. A person lets himself get arrested in order to put his father's remains in the ground."

"His *remains?*" said Osvaldo.

"Yes. Remains. What did I say wrong?"

"Nothing. It just seems like a strange choice of words for you."

"It's a perfectly normal choice of words. In any case, I was trying to say that I didn't think Michele was a pleasant person. He could be nice. He played Monopoly with Elisabetta. He helped me paint furniture. But deep down he thought I was a fool—I knew he thought it and it bothered me."

"Why are you talking about Michele in the past tense," said Osvaldo.

"Because I'm convinced he'll never come back," said Ada. "We will never see him again. He'll end up in America. Or who knows where. No one knows. The world is full of these young people who wander aimlessly from one place to another. How will they ever grow up? It's as if they're never supposed to grow up. As if they're supposed to stay the way they are forever—no house, no family, no job to go to, nothing. Some rags to wear. They were never young, never children, and so they are incapable of growing up. That girl with her baby for example. How is she going to mature? She's already old. She's a withered old seedling. She was born withered. Not physically, but morally. I could never understand why a person like you spends so much time in the company of all those withered seedlings. Maybe I'm wrong but I see better for you."

"You're wrong," said Osvaldo. "You're too optimistic about me."

"I'm temperamentally optimistic. But I'm not optimistic about these young people. I can't stand them. I think they create chaos. They seem so nice but deep down they're hatching a plan to blow us all sky high."

"That wouldn't be such a bad thing in the end," said Osvaldo. He'd put on his raincoat and was smoothing down his thin blond hair.

"You'd be happy about Elisabetta getting blown sky high?"

"Not Elisabetta," said Osvaldo.

"You need to take that raincoat to the dry cleaners," said Ada.

"Sometimes you talk to me as if we were still married," said Osvaldo. "Like just now, that's the way a wife talks."

"Do you hate it?"

"No. Why?"

"You left me. I didn't leave you. But never mind. Why drag up resentment," said Ada. "Which isn't to say you weren't right. You made a smart decision. You do well alone. And I'm terrific by myself. We weren't made to live together. We're too different."

"Too different," said Osvaldo.

"Don't repeat my words as if you were the cat in *Pinocchio*. It irritates me," said Ada. "Now I have to go to Elisabetta's school. I promised I'd dress the puppets for the Christmas Pageant. I'm taking the leftover fabric I have in the trunk."

"You're always making work for yourself," said Osvaldo. "You could stay home and relax all afternoon if you wanted. The weather's bad. Not cold, but windy."

"If I stay here all afternoon, I'll start thinking about sad things," said Ada.

"Bye," said Osvaldo.

"Bye," said Ada. "You want to know something?"

"What?"

"Deep down Michele thought you were a fool too. It wasn't just me. He sucked your blood but privately thought you were an idiot."

"Michele never sucked my blood," said Osvaldo.

He left. He hadn't brought his car and he walked back over the bridge. He stopped for a moment to look at the dense yellow water, the cars rushing, the tall plane trees. There was a furious gust of hot wind. The sky was heavy with swollen black clouds. Osvaldo thought about the machine gun Angelica had told him about after she'd thrown it into the river not far from this bridge. He'd never touched a weapon in his life. He'd never even held a fishing gun. Neither had Michele for that matter, at least not that he knew about. Michele had been exempted from the draft because of his weak lungs. And because his father had paid a bribe. Osvaldo had never done military service either because he was the only child of a widow. He'd only been a boy during the Resistance. He'd been evacuated with his mother to a town near Varese.

He ducked into a narrow alley filled with children and entered his store. Signora Peroni was carrying piles of books back and forth, limping on her massive calves. She smiled at him.

"How's it going," he said.

"She's gone back to Via dei Prefetti," she said. "No way around that. She was no help in the house. My mother ended up taking care of her plus doing all the cooking. She never remembered to dry off after a shower and left wet footprints all over the floor. The other day, she went out when both me and my mother were also out and forgot her keys and the baby was alone, crying, poor thing, and she couldn't find a locksmith so the porter called the fire department and they had to break a window to get in. My mother has become very fond of the baby. But that girl was going out too much and leaving the baby behind. My mother was always having to change him and give him his bottle."

"Forgive me," said Osvaldo. "I'll pay for the window."

"Don't think of it. We would have taken her on happily. It's a good deed. But it wasn't practical. She'd wake us up in the middle of the night to help change the baby. She said it was too sad to be alone. She'd wake us both up, me and my mother, saying that the more people there were the more comforting it was. We felt sorry for her. But it's hard to figure out why she had that baby given how unhappy it makes her to take care of him."

"It doesn't make sense," said Osvaldo. "But deep down it makes perfect sense."

"So she left today. We bundled the baby inside that big yellow bassinet so he wouldn't catch cold. We had to call her a taxi. And my mother loaned her a sweater because she didn't have anything warm to wear. She burned that kimono with the dragons—she burned it ironing."

"What a shame," said Osvaldo.

"Yes, a shame. It was a nice robe. Very charming. But she just put the iron down on top of it and went to answer the phone. Then she spent a long time on the phone. She told me it was Angelica. So now there's a big iron burn, right in the middle of the back, where the dragons are. The iron caught fire too ... for just a moment. My mother was so frightened. I worry about mother. She's old. It was all wearing her out and frightening her. If it was just me, I might have made it work."

"I understand. I'm sorry," said Osvaldo.

9

December 18, 1970

Dear Michele,

I went to see the girl on Via dei Prefetti last night. Mara ... what a silly name. Maria would have been better. Just add one "i" and everything would have been different.

I brought her a little money. I got it from Mamma. But Osvaldo says rather than give her money, we should try to help her get set up, which is not easy because she can't do anything right. Osvaldo situated her with Signora Peroni and her mother. There's another, older, Signora Peroni. She's in her eighties but still sharp. They live in Montesacro. They took in her and the baby to live there and gave her some money every month. Mara was supposed to help out a little around the house. She was only there a few days before she set the house on fire and called the fire department. At least that's what I can make out from the long, jumbled story she told me. There wasn't much to eat at the Peronis', she said. A piece of salt cod at lunch, another piece reheated with onions for dinner. Mara says she couldn't digest any of it and was living on Alka-Seltzer. She'd wake up in the middle of the night with a blinding hunger and go hunting through the house, looking for cheese. That's why her milk dried up. But Osvaldo says that she lies. It's a cute baby but not yours. He has a large mouth and long black curls. Though he might have gotten the hair from our father. She and the baby are back on Via dei Prefetti now.

That boy, Ray, you sent, stayed with me for a week but then he argued with Oreste. Ray called him a "revisionist." That made Oreste so angry he punched him. His mouth was bleeding and I was scared he'd broken his teeth. But he just split his lip a little. Me, Sonia, and Ray went down to the drugstore and Oreste stayed upstairs. He was shocked. Ray wasn't shocked, but his lip was bleeding so much that it got all over his windbreaker. The pharmacist told us not to worry and treated the cut. The next day I called Osvaldo. Now Ray is staying in your studio. Sonia brings him things to eat and things to read, newspapers and comics, because he's trying to learn how to draw comics. His friend who draws comics promised to introduce him to an editor at a newspaper. So he's endlessly sketching women with enormous breasts and enormous eyes. He saw your owl paintings and added a few owls flying around the enormous breasts.

Mamma got it into her head that Oreste had attacked Ray because he was jealous. But Oreste can't be jealous because Ray and I are basically indifferent to each other. I don't think he's especially nice. But he's not mean. He's an amoeba. According to Oreste he has fascist ideas. But Oreste sees fascists and spies everywhere. Again, there's nothing going on between me and Ray, and he had sex with Sonia in your studio in your bed under Mamma's lovely blankets. I told Mamma about it and she asked me to take the nice blankets and leave something less nice. But I don't think I'll do that because it seems unfriendly. Sometimes Mamma's ideas are unfriendly. And she has unfriendly ideas about people she's never met. If she were to meet Ray, I don't think she'd want him sleeping under ugly blankets. I washed his windbreaker thinking that it was something you could wash but it wasn't because it dried stiff, like a piece of salt cod.

I ate at Mamma's on Sunday. Oreste didn't come because there was some kind of union meeting. I brought the baby. Osvaldo was there with his daughter. Mamma has rabbits now. The girls had so much fun playing with the rabbits. I don't know how they managed to have so much fun because they're not fun rabbits, they sleep all the time. The twins pulled them out of their cages by the ears. They lounged on the grass and didn't even try to escape. They're the kind that shed a lot. The twins spent hours picking fur off their jackets. It was a beautiful sunny day. Mamma seemed depressed.

I think our father's death has crushed her. I think it brought back all those years they were together. She's always on the verge of tears, always getting up and leaving the room. She took father's painting of her sitting at the window in the house at Pieve di Cadore and hung it in the living room. You won't remember because you were little but I remember everything. That was an awful summer. They'd stopped fighting but there was something in the air, a sense that something was about to happen. Sometimes I could hear Mamma crying at night.

I don't know who was right or wrong. I don't even wonder. I only know that waves of unhappiness streamed out of their bedroom into the whole house. There wasn't a corner of the house spared. There was unhappiness everywhere. We had so much fun in that house for so many summers. It was a beautiful house. There were so many places to play, the woodshed, so many nooks to hide in, turkeys in the yard. You wouldn't remember. Then Cecilia came and took us to Chianciano. After a few weeks our father arrived and told us they were separating. He told us that you would be staying with him. Us girls with

62

Mamma. No explanations. That was what they'd decided. He stayed in Chianciano for two or three days. He sat out in the hotel lobby, smoking and drinking Martinis. When Cecilia spoke to him he told her to shut up.

Maybe Mamma is still in love with Filippo. I don't know. They were together for years and I think she always assumed he would come live with her. Instead he got married to someone who's younger than I am. He didn't have the courage to tell Mamma about the marriage and asked me to be there with him. Filippo is not a brave man. It was a horrendous morning. That was last May. I remember it was May because the trellis under the windows in Via dei Villini was full of roses.

Mamma is really very lonely now. The twins pay no attention to her. You're not here. Viola and I have our own things to take care of. She's alone with Matilde and Matilde drives her crazy. But at least there's someone, a presence in the house, a voice, footsteps in the empty rooms. I have no idea why Mamma bought that enormous house. She must regret it. She probably also regrets having asked Matilde to live there, even though she knows that total solitude would be worse. But Matilde really gets on her nerves. Matilde calls her "Little Bear" and keeps asking "How are you?" while stroking her chin and looking into her eyes. Every morning she goes into Mamma's room to do yoga in her bathing suit because she says it's the only warm spot in the house. There's no way Mamma has it in her to ask her to leave, she becomes a meek lamb. She's even taken to sitting and listening to Matilde read to her aloud from her novel *Polenta and Poison*. Matilde dug it out of her suitcase and wants to revise it now because Osvaldo thoughtlessly mentioned that Ada is close with a book editor. His name is Colarosa. He has a very small publishing house. I think he's Ada's boyfriend. Matilde is consumed with the idea of this editor. She reads *Polenta and Poison* out loud every night to Mamma and Osvaldo, who's there almost every evening. He and Mamma have become pretty good friends. There's nothing sexual between them, naturally. I don't think Osvaldo is interested in women. I have this notion he's a repressed pedophile. I also have a notion that he is subconsciously in love with you. I don't know what you think but it's what I think.

I'd love to see you again. I'm doing well. Flora started school. She eats lunch there and comes home at four. Sonia has been picking her up because I'm usually in the office until seven. My work is still dreary and ridiculous. Right now, I have to translate a long article about water contamination. I get home and go shopping, make dinner, iron Oreste's shirts because he won't wear the ones that don't need ironing. After that he goes into the office and I fall asleep in front of the television.

Angelica

Ti abbraccio

10

"I THINK SHE'S utterly stupid," said Mara.

"You're wrong," said Osvaldo.

"Utterly," said Mara.

"She has moments of great insight and wisdom—she does. She's limited, of course. No matter what, she's my wife and I'd like you stop calling her names. I've been here for a quarter of an hour and you haven't talked about anything else."

"You're split up. She's not your wife anymore."

"It still bugs me when people talk poorly of her in front of me."

"Does that happen often?"

"What do you care?"

"I don't think she's pretty or elegant."

"She actually is pretty and can be quite elegant."

"She wasn't elegant yesterday. Or the other time. She's always wearing the same fur. American wolf. The streets must be full of wolves over there. Wolves everywhere. I couldn't even see her body because she was covered in so much fur. She has nice calves but her knees are fat. And the huge tortoiseshell glasses. Why doesn't she get the glasses with invisible frames? She had a little mustache. It's bleached, but I could see it. She came in here and kept her hands in her pockets. She was judging me, the baby, the apartment. When you asked her if she'd seen how big the baby had gotten she said he was cute. The same way you'd say a lamp was cute. She wasn't polite at all."

"Ada is shy, underneath" said Osvaldo.

"The way you see it they're all shy. You told me that if she ever came here the first thing she'd do would be to summon electricians and contractors. She didn't summon anyone. She hasn't lifted a finger. All she had to say was that it smells like a sewer. I already know that."

"She didn't say it smells like a sewer, she said you could smell the courtyard, or something like that."

"I am at war with the smell of this house and nothing works. Some houses smell and this is a smelly house. I bleach, use ammonia. You have no idea how much money I've spent here. She didn't have any wonderful advice. She just recommended a dish rack. What an insight!"

"Did you buy it?"

"No. I didn't have time. I've been taking care of those damn Peroni ladies the whole week. They aren't mean, actually, they were nice. But they made my milk dry up with all the salt cod. I got back here and the ceiling had flooded. I called a handyman. I called the handyman, not your wife. All sorts of things had gone wrong. I'm so worried I'm not going to be able to stay here. My friend, the one who loaned me the apartment, came over the other day with a Japanese friend. They say they want to start an 'Oriental boutique' in here. I told them that I didn't think the apartment was suitable, it's the top floor, there's no elevator, and it smells like a sewer. The Japanese guy was friendly enough, and he said I could be a 'vendeuse' in the boutique. My friend said that no matter what, boutique or not, she's going to want the apartment back because she needs money. Then we had a fight and it ended badly. The Japanese guy was still nice to me and said he'll get me a kimono because I told him how my other one got burned. If she kicks me out, I don't know where I'll go. It's true that I could always go live in the famous *studio*. Michele isn't coming back anytime soon."

"The studio belongs to Ada. I don't know what her plans are. She might want to rent it out."

"Good God, you people are attached to money. I can't pay rent. Maybe eventually. The studio is pretty dark and it's probably damp too. But I could work with that. It would be convenient because you're right upstairs and I could call you at night if I needed something."

"I aspire to not be woken in the night," said Osvaldo.

11

December 29, 1970

Dear Michele,

Your sister Angelica came to see me. I'd never met her before. She is nice and very pretty. She gave me money. Sixty thousand lire. I can't do anything with sixty thousand lire, but it was a nice gesture. I know that you told her to give me money. Thank you. I told your sister that I would go visit your mother one day. She says that your mother has been very depressed lately but that soon, when she's less depressed, I can go see her.

Angelica gave me your address because I wanted to send my condolences to you. I can say Merry Christmas and Happy New Year while I'm at it. Of course Christmas has passed. I was sad and alone on Christmas day, the baby was crying and had a stuffy nose. But later in the day a Japanese guy I know brought me a kimono. It's black with two giant sunflowers, one on the front and one on the back.

I have good news. I found a job. I've already started. I take the baby to a lady to be looked after and she keeps him until six. I pick him up on my way home. She costs twenty thousand lire a month. Ada, Osvaldo's wife, got me the job. She also found me the lady who takes care of the baby. I think Ada is a fool, but she's been very nice to me.

I'm working for an editor, named Fabio Colarosa. He's Ada's friend. They might be sleeping together. It's not totally clear. Osvaldo says it's possible they've been sleeping together for two years now. He is short and thin and has a huge round nose. He looks like a pelican. The office is on Via Po. I sit all alone in one big room. Colarosa sits all alone in another big room. He sits at his desk thinking. When he thinks, he wrinkles up his nose and his lips. Sometimes he talks into his Dictaphone. He'll shut his eyes and stroke his hair, very, very slowly. I type his letters and anything else he says on the Dictaphone. Occasionally he'll put thoughts on the Dictaphone. Complicated thoughts that I don't entirely understand. I'm also supposed to answer the telephone but no one ever calls except sometimes Ada. There's another big room where two boys work, they box the books and design covers. We are going to publish your Aunt Matilde's book. It's called *Polenta and Wine*, or something like that. They've already designed the cover. It has a sun and some piles of dirt with a hoe sticking out of one, because the book is about a peasant girl. The two boys say that the cover looks like a socialist political poster. Your mother put up the money for the book. Not as if I needed the money or anything, because I do. I make fifty thousand lire a month there. What can I do with fifty thousand lire a month? Nothing. But Colarosa told me he'd give me a raise. He says he doesn't care that I can't speak English.

Osvaldo said that it took him two days to convince Ada to recommend me to Colarosa. When she did recommend me to him, she told him I was crazy. He told her he didn't have any problem with crazy people. I think that's a great response.

At noon every day, I go down to the cafe and get a cappuccino and sandwich. The other day Colarosa saw me heading to the cafe and invited me to go with him to a restaurant. He's a quiet type, but not like the totally silent kind of person who makes you uncomfortable. He asks the occasional question and when he listens to the answer he wrinkles his nose and mouth. I had a fun lunch. I don't know why it was so fun since he barely said a word. He told me that the Dictaphone thoughts are notes for a book. I asked him if your Aunt Matilde's book is any good and he said it was a pile of garbage. But he took it on as a favor to Ada, who wanted to do a favor for Osvaldo who wanted to do a favor for your aunt, etc., etc. In the end, your mother was the one who put up all the money.

The baby looks like you. His hair is black and straight and yours is curly and practically red but children's hair changes and might grow out differently. His eyes are the color of lead. Yours are green but I've heard that even eye color can change. I'd like it if he was yours but I'm not sure. But you shouldn't think that I'll try to make you the father when you come back. I'd be a fool to do that to you and also an asshole since I'm not even sure you're the father. As it stands, this baby will have no father and sometimes that feels really heavy, but then other times I feel okay about it and think everything will turn out fine.

You and I had fun together. I don't know why it was fun, but then who ever knows why one person bores you and another one doesn't. There were times when it seemed like you were really fed up and you didn't want to talk to me. I'd ask you something and instead of answering you'd just grunt, you could do it without even moving your lips. When I miss you now, I just make that sound and you appear before me. You were really fed up the whole time toward the end. Maybe I was being clingy. But I didn't want anything from you. I just wanted your company. Honestly, I never wanted you to marry me. Just the idea of us getting married makes me laugh, and gives me chills. If I ever had that idea in my head, I banished it totally.

You really hurt my feelings that one time you arrived for our date, and you were out of breath and pale. You told me you'd run over a nun. Later, when we were back at the studio you told me she was dead. You buried your head in the pillow and I comforted you. The next morning you wouldn't talk to me and when I touched your hair you made that throat grunt and pulled away. You have an ugly side, but that's not why I don't want to marry you. I don't want to marry you because you hurt me that time and a lot of other times too, and I want to get married to a man who won't hurt me because I'm already good at hurting myself. I want to marry a man that I can look up to.

I'm sending you a hug and I'll write again.

Mara

12

January 6, 1971

Dear Michele,

How wonderful to talk to you on the phone. I could hear your voice so clearly. Osvaldo is such a nice person, coming to get me and letting me call you from his house. And that way he could say hello too.

I was so pleased to hear about your walks in the woods with all those dogs. I can imagine you now, hiking in the woods. I'm glad I remembered to send your boots because the grass must be wet and muddy. I have woods around here too, if you climb high enough up the hill, and every so often Matilde proposes a walk up there, but the mere idea of seeing her Tyrolese scarf blowing in the wind ahead of me makes me lose any desire to take a walk. Even when I'm alone I never feel like going up into the woods and the twins never want to come walking with me either. I end up looking at the woods from the window and it seems like it's a faraway place. Maybe a person needs to be peaceful, generally happy, to enjoy walking in the countryside. I hope to be a person like that one day and hope you already are.

But I still don't understand what you think you're doing. Osvaldo says I should leave you be. You're learning English and you're passing the time doing housework, which, according to him, is always useful. I do want to know though when you're planning on coming back.

Osvaldo and I went over to the studio to collect your paintings. That friend of yours, Ray, was there. He's living in the workshop now, as you know. Angelica's friend Sonia was there too, the one with the black ponytail. There were other people. Maybe a dozen. They were sitting on your bed and on the floor. The door was open and we walked right in but no one moved, they just kept doing what they were doing, which is to say, nothing. Sonia helped us carry the paintings to the car. No one else lifted a finger. As soon as I got home I hung up all of your paintings. I don't think they're the least bit beautiful, but then in a way, it's better that they aren't any good, since you've stopped painting. Osvaldo thinks you've stopped forever. Who knows what you'll do next. Osvaldo says I shouldn't worry about it. You'll do something.

It was very depressing to see the studio again. I got the sense it depressed Osvaldo to be there too. The bed was out and there were the blankets that I'd bought you. Why should I care about these blankets. But I had told Angelica to take them for herself, it's not like she's drowning in nice bedding.

Matilde and I spent Christmas alone. The twins went skiing at Campo Imperatore. Angelica and Oreste were with their friends, the Bettoias, who I don't know. Viola and Elio were in the country with his family. Nonetheless, Matilde and I prepared a sort of Christmas dinner, even if it was just the two of us eating alone in the kitchen. Cloti went home for the holiday and we didn't think she'd ever come back because she took almost all of her clothes with her. Matilde made capon stuffed with raisins and chestnuts, and she made a bavarese too. So after dinner the kitchen was filled with dirty dishes, as our dishwasher is broken, and Matilde went to sleep, saying that the twins could wash the dishes when they came back. Matilde has these fantasies about the twins. I washed and dried the dishes. Osvaldo and his daughter Elisabetta appeared in the afternoon along with their dog. I offered them the leftover bavarese. The girl wouldn't touch the bavarese and settled down to read the twins' comic books. Osvaldo fixed the dishwasher. Just when they were about to leave Matilde emerged from her room and got angry because I hadn't woken her. She said she'd fallen asleep out of pure boredom since no one ever comes visiting in this house. She insisted they stay for supper, and they did. And so there were more dishes to wash and the dishwasher broke again right away, flooding the kitchen floor. Against all expectations, Cloti reappeared the next day. She brought us a bushel of apples that Matilde has claimed as her own. She takes enormous bites out of these apples and claims that she should eat an apple every half hour for her health.

Osvaldo comes by almost every evening. Matilde thinks he's in love with me, but Matilde is a half-wit. I think it's sheer inertia that brings him here, force of habit. In the beginning he was coming to listen to Matilde read from *Polenta and Poison*, but now, as God is merciful, that has ended. Matilde would read aloud in a deep, throaty voice and Osvaldo and I would sit there, cynical and jaded. Now Osvaldo has passed her along to an editor friend of Ada's. I'll cover the expenses. Matilde asked me to and I didn't know how to refuse.

I don't understand your Osvaldo. He isn't unpleasant, but he irks me. He sits here until midnight, leafing through magazines. We don't talk much. Usually he'll wait for me to start the conversation. I make some effort but we don't have much in common. Back when there was *Polenta and Poison* to listen to, we slept, but that was a reason to sit together. Now I don't see any reason to be sitting together. And yet I have to admit that I'm happy when he shows up. I've come to depend on it. When I see him at the door I feel a strange sense of relief mixed with irritation.

Your mother
Ti abbraccio

I asked Osvaldo if that girl Mara Pastorelli was in the studio when we went to get your paintings. He said she wasn't. They aren't her friends, they run in different circles. I sent her money through Angelica. She and Osvaldo thought we should send money because she's not doing well, and there's that poor baby. Now they got her a job with Ada's editor friend. This Ada is always so helpful.

13

January 8, 1971

Dear Michele,

Yesterday was the reading of your father's will. Lillino had been holding onto it. Your father wrote it right after he got sick. I knew nothing about it. Me, Lillino, Matilde, Angelica, Elio, and Viola were all in the lawyer's office. Oreste didn't come because he had a work conflict at the newspaper.

Your father left you a series of paintings, the ones he did between 1945 and 1955, and the Via San Sebastianello house, and the tower. I get the impression your sisters are going to come out of this with much less than you. They'll get those properties near Spoleto, many of which have been sold off, but there are some left. Matilde and Cecilia are going to get a piece of furniture, that baroque, Piemonte credenza. Matilde immediately observed that Cecilia gets the better end of that deal because Matilde wouldn't know what to do with a credenza. Can you just imagine. What joy will half-blind, decrepit Cecilia get from a credenza?

As for the Via San Sebastianello house, you'll need to let us know what you want to do about it: sell it, rent it, or live there. The architect has already begun work on the tower, so that's all set. There are huge expenses associated with the projects your father contracted. Lillino says that he and I should go to the tower to see what's already been done. Lillino has never seen the tower but says that there's no way it was a good investment because you can't get there by car unless you build a road into the rock. The only way to get there now is via a steep footpath along the cliff. I have little desire to go rock climbing with Lillino.

I wish you would come here and decide. I can't make these decisions for you. How could I decide anything if I have no idea where and how you want to live.

Your mother

14

January 12, 1971

Dear Mamma,

Thank you for your letters. I'm writing quickly because I'm leaving Sussex and heading to Leeds with a girl I met. She has a job teaching design at a school in Leeds. I think I'll be able to get work washing dishes and servicing the boiler at the school. I've become very proficient at servicing boilers and washing dishes.

I'm leaving on good terms with the nice couple I live with here, the professor and his wife. He's a little queer, but just a little. He taught me to play the clarinet.

Leeds isn't much of a city. I saw some postcards. The girl I'm going with isn't much either. She's a little boring, but not stupid. I'm going with her because I've had enough of things here.

I'm asking you to please send me some money in Leeds as soon as possible. I still don't know exactly where I'll be staying, but you could send the money in the care of this girl's mother. I'm putting her address below. And can you also do me the favor of sending Kant's *Prolegomena to Any Future Metaphysics* to the same address too. It's in the studio. I can find it here, but it's in English. They might have an Italian version in the library, but I can't stand libraries. Thank you.

I can't come back now. To be honest, I don't want to come back. I could come back if I wanted to, but don't. Why don't you go live in the San Sebastianello house since from your letters you sound bored and depressed in the country.

You decide about the tower. I don't think I'll ever go regardless of the season.

If you don't want to move to San Sebastianello, maybe you can let Mara Pastorelli, the girl, my friend, live there. She's the girl you sent money to. She is living in an apartment on Via dei Prefetti, but it might be uncomfortable there. The San Sebastianello house is very comfortable. I have good memories from there.

Congratulate Matilde for me on her novel, *Polenta and Wine*, which I understand is about to be published. Hug the twins and everyone else for me.

Michele

Write me c/o Mrs. Thomas, 52 Bedford Road, Leeds

15

January 15, 1971

Dear Michele,

Something very weird happened and I feel like I need to tell you about it right away. Yesterday me and Fabio had sex. Fabio Colarosa, the editor. He's the pelican. You have no idea how much he looks like a pelican. He's Ada's boyfriend. I stole him from Ada.

He invited me to the restaurant. Then he brought me home because it was a holiday and the office was closed for the afternoon. He said he wanted to come up and meet the baby. Ada had told him about the baby. I explained to him that the baby wasn't home, he was with the lady. He said he wanted to see my house. I was embarrassed about the sewer smell that's always there. And when I went to work that morning I had left everything out. But he was insistent so I let him come up. He sat on the only chair, the one with the torn cushion. I made him a Nescafé. I served it to him in the pink plastic mug that my friend at the boardinghouse had given me. I don't have any other mugs. I always mean to go to the store to get some more, but never have the time. After he drank his coffee he started pacing, back and forth, and wrinkling his nose. I asked him if he could smell the stench. He said he couldn't. He said he has a big nose but can't smell much. I had made the bed and was sitting on it, and he sat down next to me and that's how we ended up having sex. I was really shocked afterward. But he fell asleep. I watched his big nose sleeping. I said, "Jesus Christ, I'm in bed with the pelican."

It was five and I had to go pick up the baby. He woke up while I was dressing. He said he wanted to stay for a while longer. I left and came back with the baby. He was still there, lying in the bed, he poked his nose out of the sheets to look at the baby and said he was handsome. Then he lay back down. I prepared the baby's bottle and was happy to have him there because I don't like to be alone when I mix the milk. I should be used to it by now because I'm almost always alone, but I'm not used to it. I had a veal chop for dinner, I cooked it and we each ate half. While we were eating I told him that he looked exactly like a pelican. He said he'd heard that before. He didn't remember who'd told him that. I said, "Maybe it was Ada," I could tell he didn't really want to talk about Ada, but I did. I didn't tell him that I think she's a fool. I told him that I thought she was a little insufferable. He started laughing. I asked him if he'd had enough to eat. He said pelicans don't eat much. He stayed the whole night. He got dressed and left in the morning. Then we saw each other back at the office. He was sitting there with his Dictaphone. He winked at me when I came in. But I didn't say anything. He was formal with me. I figured he wanted to pretend nothing had happened at the office. He didn't invite me out to the restaurant. Ada picked him up. Now I'm hungry because I've only had half a veal chop, two cappuccinos, and a sandwich since last night. Now I'm going to go down and buy some ham.

I don't know when he'll be back. He didn't tell me when he'd be back. I have this feeling I'm in love. I don't feel sorry for him the way I sometimes feel sorry for you. I envy him. I envy the dreamy way he has, he's strange and mysterious. You are sometimes dreamy and strange and mysterious too, but all of your secrets seem like a children's game. He seems to have real secrets, secrets he'll never tell anyone, complicated and strange secrets. I envy him. Because I don't even have half a secret.

It's been a long time since I've had sex. Not since the baby was born. Partly it's that no one's come along. Partly it's that I haven't been interested. The Japanese man is queer. I wouldn't dream of having sex with Osvaldo. He might be queer too and I'm not attracted to him, I don't know.

Angelica is going to pick me up and take me to see a friend of hers who has a stroller. It's stored under the stairs and she doesn't need it anymore. Angelica says we'll have to clean it with Lysol.

I don't know if I'll tell Angelica about the pelican. I don't know her well and what if she gets the impression that I just go to bed with the first guy I see. But maybe I will tell her because I'm dying to tell her. I'll tell Osvaldo as soon as I see him for sure. I stole Ada's pelican.

Ti abbraccio.
Mara

Angelica arrived. We went to get the stroller. It's a very good stroller. I told Angelica everything while we were walking.

Angelica gave me your new address. She told me about Leeds, the city you've moved to, how it's gray and very boring. What the hell are you going to do in Leeds? Angelica says that you moved to Leeds to be with a girl. I was jealous right away of this girl. I don't care about you at all, I just have feelings of friendship toward you, but still I'm jealous of all your girls.

16

ANGELICA WOKE UP. It was Sunday. The baby was staying with friends for two days. Oreste was in Orvieto. She walked barefoot around the house, opening shutters. It was a damp, sunny morning. The scent from the pastry shop in the square drifted up. She found her green terry slippers in the kitchen and slid them onto her feet. She found her white shower cap on the typewriter in the dining room and stuffed her hair in it. After her shower, she put on a red bathrobe, damp because Oreste had used it the night before. She made tea. She sat in the kitchen drinking tea and reading yesterday's newspaper. She pulled off the shower cap and her hair fell out over her shoulders. She went to get dressed. She looked in her drawer for stockings but they all had runs. She dug out a pair that had a hole in the heel, but no runs. She pulled on a pair of boots. While she was buckling the boots it occurred to her that she didn't love Oreste anymore. The idea that he would be in Orvieto for the whole day gave her a deep sense of freedom. And he didn't love her anymore. She thought he was in love with the girl who wrote the women's page at the newspaper. Then she thought that probably none of this was true. She pulled on a blue sweater and scraped at a white spot on her skirt with her fingernail. It was flour and milk. She had made apple fritters the night before with Oreste and the Bettoias. While they were eating the fritters she put her head on Oreste's shoulder and he hugged her for moment. Then he shrugged her off, saying he was hot. He took off his jacket and scolded her for putting the thermostat up too high. The Bettoias were hot too. The fritters were greasy. She stood in front of the mirror and pulled back her hair to study her long, pale, serious face.

The doorbell rang. It was Viola. She was wearing a new coat, black with a leopard trim. She had a leopard beret on her head. Her black hair hung loose over her shoulders, straight and shiny. Her eyes were brown with blue flecks, her nose small and delicate. Her mouth was small and her upper lip poked out over big white teeth. She took off her jacket and placed it carefully on the dresser in the entryway. Under the coat she was wearing a red scoop-neck sweater. Angelica poured tea. Viola wrapped her hands around the mug because she was cold. She asked Angelica why the heat was turned down so low.

She'd come over to say that she thought the will was wrong. Mostly she didn't think it was fair that their father had left that tower to Michele. She and Elio had been thinking the tower would be a lovely place for the sisters to go in the summertime. Michele wasn't going to do anything with the tower. Angelica said that she hadn't seen the tower but knew that they would need to spend a lot of money she didn't have in order to make it habitable. Anyway the tower belonged to Michele. "Fool," said Viola. "We just need to sell some of that land in Spoleto to get the money for the tower." She asked for a cracker, because she had skipped breakfast. Angelica didn't have any crackers but she had some broken breadsticks in a plastic bag. Viola started eating the breadsticks, dunking them in tea. She thought she might be pregnant, she was ten days late. That morning she felt strangely slow. "You don't feel anything in the first days," said

Angelica. "I'll take the rabbit test tomorrow," said Viola. She calculated that the baby would be born in early August. "The worst month to have a baby," she said. "I'll die from the heat. It'll be awful." In two years they would be able to all vacation together in the tower. Elio would collect mussels from the rocks. He loved to collect mussels. They would eat marvelous mussel soup together. They would get a grill to cook steak outside. Oreste and Elio could go spear fishing. Then they could have grouper on the grill instead of steak. "Oreste has never been spear fishing," said Angelica. The phone rang, and Angelica went to answer. It was Osvaldo. He told her that Ray had been hit on the head during a protest and was injured. They were at the Polyclinic, could she come.

Angelica put on her jacket and asked Viola for a ride because she didn't have her car, Oreste had taken it. On the stairs, Viola said she didn't want to give Angelica a ride. She wasn't feeling well. She felt tired. Angelica said she'd take a taxi but then, as she was getting into the taxi, Viola changed her mind and said she'd take them after all. The driver cursed at them.

When they were in the car, Viola started talking about the tower again. They could put a lookout on the top, and she could take the baby up there. The air density would be so marvelous up there. "Why would the air density be so much more marvelous up there," said Angelica. "It gets hot on the Isola del Giglio. The sun will be beating down on you, on the lookout, and the baby will roast alive." "We'll put up a canopy," said Viola. "And we can put down paving stones in all the rooms to keep it cool. They are easier to wash than ceramic and less fragile." Angelica said that she thought she remembered their father had already selected and purchased a vast quantity of ceramic tiles. Anyway, the tower belonged to Michele. "Michele will never go there," said Viola. "He'll never get married. Michele will never have a family of his own. He's gay." "You wish he was," said Angelica. "He's a homosexual," said Viola. "Haven't you figured out that he and Osvaldo were lovers?" "You wish," said Angelica. While she was saying, "you wish," she realized that it was exactly what she'd always thought. "Michele had a girlfriend, and he's probably the father of her baby," she said. "Because he's bisexual," said Viola. "Osvaldo has a daughter," said Angelica. "Is he bisexual too?" "Bisexual," said Viola.

"Poor Michele," said Viola. "It hurts my heart to think of Michele." "I don't feel sorry for Michele at all," said Angelica. "It makes me happy to think of him." But, really, she felt like her heart was being squeezed and she felt generally undone. "Michele is in Leeds with a girl now," she said. "I know," said Viola. "He's never happy. He goes from one place to another. He tries one thing then another. Our father destroyed him. He spoiled him. He took him away from us and from our mother. He neglected Michele. He doted on him and neglected him. He always left him alone in the house with that old cook. And that's why Michele turned homosexual. Out of loneliness. He missed his mother and sisters and that turns you homosexual—when you think of women as something absent but desired. My therapist told me that. You know I have a therapist." "I know," said Angelica. "I was having trouble sleeping," said Viola. "I was anxious. I sleep much better now that I see a therapist." "Either way, Michele is not homosexual," said Angelica. "And he's not bisexual. He's straight. And even if he is bisexual I don't see why that means we should take his tower away from him."

Viola said she'd go with them into the hospital for a while. They found Osvaldo, Sonia, and Ada waiting outside the emergency room. Osvaldo had asked Ada to come because she had a doctor friend who worked at the hospital. Sonia was carrying Ray's windbreaker over her arm. She'd been next to him when they'd thrown him to the ground. She saw the people who did it. They were Fascists. They had chains. Ada saw her doctor friend pass by and ran after him. The doctor reassured them that Ray hadn't been hurt badly and he could go home.

Viola and Ada went to get something to eat. Ada ordered a coffee and Viola a hot toddy. Viola said she was going to leave because her knees were trembling. Hospitals scared her and this was all upsetting. She'd seen a nurse carrying a bucket of bloody gauze walk past. She was worried she'd have a miscarriage. Ada asked how far along she was. A month, answered Viola. Ada said that when she was seven months pregnant she spent many nights on end in the hospital looking after one of her maids who had peritonitis.

Ray came out of the emergency room with a bandaged head. Viola and Ada left. Sonia and Angelica helped Ray into Osvaldo's Fiat. They drove to Osvaldo's house. Ray lay down on the couch in the parlor. It was a big parlor with couches and armchairs. All the upholstery was worn and frayed. Osvaldo brought in a bottle of Lambrusco. Angelica drank a glass of Lambrusco and curled up on a chair, resting her head on the arm. She watched Osvaldo and Sonia come and go to the kitchen. She looked at Osvaldo's broad back in his camel-colored sweater, his big square head and thin blond hair. She felt happy to be there with Osvaldo, Sonia, and Ray, and happy that Viola and Ada had left. She felt that life was sweet. She thought maybe Viola was right about Osvaldo. Maybe he was Michele's lover, but it was hard to imagine and it didn't matter anyway. Ray had fallen asleep with a plaid blanket pulled up over his head. Osvaldo brought in a big pot and set it on the glass coffee table by the couch. Sonia carried bowls. Ray woke and they ate spaghetti with olive oil, garlic, and hot pepper. They spent the afternoon smoking, listening to records, drinking Lambrusco, and making occasional comments. When it got dark, Ray went back down to the studio and Sonia followed him.

Angelica had to go home and Osvaldo took her. He didn't feel like being alone yet, he said—they had spent such a wonderful afternoon, the four of them, doing nothing.

At home, Angelica stood at the window, waiting for her daughter to be dropped off. Osvaldo found a book on the typewriter and started reading. The title was *Ten Days That Shook the World*. Angelica saw her daughter climbing out of the car. She waved at the friends who had hosted her. Her daughter was happy and tired. They had gone to Anzio and she played outside in the pine forest. She'd already eaten at a restaurant. Angelica watched her undress and helped her button up her pajamas. She turned off the light and kissed the blonde hair spilling out over the covers. She went to the kitchen, got a knife and newspaper, and scraped the mud off the child's shoes. She found some peas to reheat and dressed them with chopped leftover ham. Oreste would be home late. She sat in a chair near Osvaldo, pulled off her boots, and looked at the hole in her stocking, which had gotten bigger. Osvaldo was still reading. She rested her head on the arm of the chair and fell asleep. She dreamed of the word *bisexual*. In the dream, the word and bits of ceramic tiles were scattered in a pine forest. The telephone rang and woke her up. It was Elio. He begged her to come if she could. Viola was bleeding. She was in tears and wanted someone. Elio said that Angelica had been reckless to drag her to the hospital. She'd gotten worked up and was having a miscarriage. Maybe it wasn't a miscarriage said Angelica, maybe she was just menstruating. It's probably a miscarriage Elio said and Viola is devastated because she wanted the baby so very badly. Angelica buckled her boots back up and asked Osvaldo to stay until Oreste got back. She left the house and went to Viola.

17

February 15, 1971—Leeds

Dear Angelica,

I'm writing with some news that might shock you. I'm getting married. Can you please go to the office in Piazza San Silvestro to get the documents I need. I don't know which ones they want. I'm going to get married as soon as I have the papers.

I'm marrying a girl I met in Leeds. She's not actually a girl, because she's divorced and has two children. She's American. She teaches nuclear physics. The children are sweet. I love children. Not when they're very little, but once they get to be six or seven like these ones. We are having so much fun. I won't tell you all about this girl I'm marrying. She's thirty. She's not beautiful. She wears glasses. She's very intelligent. I love intelligence.

It looks like I'll be able to find work. They are looking for an Italian teacher in a private school for girls here in Leeds. I've been washing dishes up until now in another private school for girls, where Josephine, who I came here with, is a teacher. You can still write me in care of Josephine's mother. I don't have an apartment yet but I'm looking. Eileen, the girl I'm marrying, lives with her parents and children in a small house. There's no room for me. For now I'm staying in a boardinghouse but I won't give you the address because I'm moving.

I might write Mamma too, but in the meantime, will you start breaking the news to her? Tell her gradually because this is the sort of thing that might upset her. Tell her not to be upset because I've thought it through. Maybe we'll come to Italy for the Easter vacation and that way you can meet Eileen and the children.

I'm sending you a hug. Get me that paperwork quickly.

Michele

18

February 15, 1971

Dear Mara,

I'm writing to let you know that I'm getting married. The woman I'm marrying is extraordinary. She's the most intelligent woman I've ever met.

Write me. Your letters make me laugh. I read them to Eileen. Eileen, my wife. I mean, she *will* be my wife in twenty days, I just need to sort out the paperwork. We laughed like crazy about you and the pelican.

I'm sending you a pack of twelve terry onesies for the baby. Eileen wanted you to have them. They belonged to her children and she kept them. She says they are extremely handy. They are machine washable. Although, you might not have a washing machine.

Can you store them when you're done too? I might need them back in case me and Eileen have children. Eileen told me to tell you that you shouldn't throw them away.

Congratulations on your pelican.

Michele

19

February 15, 1971

Dear Osvaldo,

I'm sorry for not having written since I left. The conversation we had when you called to tell me my father had died was brief. And then we talked the time my mother was at your house. I know that I should have written and told you all about myself, given you all the news.

I hear that you see a lot of my loved ones, you spend evenings with my mother and see my sisters. This makes me very happy.

I have news that will surprise you. I've decided to get married. I'm marrying a girl named Eileen Robson. She's divorced. She has two children. She's not pretty. She's almost ugly from certain angles. She's very thin and has freckles everywhere. She wears giant glasses, like Ada. But she's not as good looking as Ada. Maybe she's what you'd call a type.

She is very intelligent. Her intelligence fascinates me and I find it reassuring. This might be because I'm not very intelligent, but I'm sharp and practical. So I know what intelligence is and I know that I don't have it. I wrote "sharp and practical" because that's how you once described me.

I could never live with a stupid woman. I may not be very intelligent, but I love and admire intelligence.

In my studio, in the bottom drawer of the bureau I think, there's a scarf. It's a beautiful scarf, white with light-blue stripes and it's real cashmere. It was a present from my father. It would make me happy if you were to get it and wear it. I would be happy to know that you were wearing that scarf when you walk along the Lungotevere, coming home from the store. I haven't forgotten our long walks along the Lungotevere, back and forth, under the setting sun.

Michele

20

February 22, 1971

Dear Michele,

The cashmere scarf cannot be found. But I bought a scarf for myself. I don't think it's cashmere and it doesn't have blue stripes, it's just white. I wear it and imagine it's yours. I am aware that it's a surrogate. But for what it's worth, we all live with surrogates.

I go see your mother often, she is very nice, and I also see, as you've heard, your friends.

As for everything else. My life is the same. Still the same. I go to the shop, I listen to Signora Peroni complain about her varicose veins and arthritis, I go through the register receipts, I talk to the few customers who come in, I take Elisabetta to gymnastics and go pick her up, I walk along the Lungotevere, I put my hands in my pockets and lean against the railing of the bridge and I watch the sun set.

I send huge congratulations on your wedding and I sent you a gift of a special, red leather-bound edition of *Fleurs du mal*.

Osvaldo

21

February 23, 1971

Dear Michele,

Angelica is over and she tells me you're getting married. She says that you told her to break the news to me gradually so that I wouldn't be upset. But she told me everything the minute she arrived. Angelica knows me better than you do. She knows I'm always upset, so that nothing new upsets me anymore. It might seem strange to you but I'm not surprised either. I'm neither shocked nor surprised by anything anymore because I'm in a perpetual state of shock and surprise.

I've been sick in bed for the last ten days. That's why I haven't written you. I called Doctor Bovo, who looked after your father, he lives on San Sebastianello on the fourth floor. I have pleurisy. It feels quite odd to write, "I have pleurisy," because I've never had anything in my life and I've always considered myself robust. Getting sick is something that happens to other people.

Angelica let me read your letter. There are certain sentences that puzzle me, despite the fact that I am, as I said, at this point essentially immune to shock. "I love intelligence." "I love children." To be perfectly honest, I didn't have the slightest idea that you loved intelligence and children. Such claims, however, leave a positive impression. It is as if you were finally seeking clarity and resolution. As if you were finally trying to make real choices.

I will be so excited to see you at Easter, to meet your wife and these children of hers. The prospect of having children in the house makes me tired just thinking about it. But since I'll be seeing you again, I welcome it all with great pleasure.

I don't think it's necessarily a bad thing that you're marrying a woman who is thirty years old. Apparently you need to have an older woman around you. You need maternal affection. This is because when you were little, your father took you away from me, God forgive him, if God exists, which is a possibility I won't exclude. I sometimes think about how little time we've spent together, you and me, and how little we know each other. I think about how superficially we pass judgment on each other. I think you're a moron. But I don't know if you're a moron. Maybe you're secretly wise.

It seems that they're finally going to install a telephone line here, thanks to Ada, who went in person to the telephone company the moment she heard I was sick.

I forgot to tell you something important. Osvaldo says that Ada would be delighted to buy your tower. That would be positive, because it would free you of the burden, even though, let's be honest, you're not in the least worried about the tower. Viola and Elio had wanted to buy it from you but then they went to see it and were disappointed. They say it's problematic to get to, the path there is steep. The tower itself looks like it would crumble if you touched it. That architect hasn't done any of the work yet. All they did was to bring a couple of contractors out there and they took out a sink and knocked down a wall. Now the sink is in the yard, dumped in the middle of a nettle patch. Your father chose new tiles and he paid for them, but they are still in the warehouse and the warehouse wants them out. Ada says the architect is a total idiot. She went with her own architect to see the tower for herself. She wants to put in a pool, install stairs down to the ocean, put in a road. We discovered that your father paid ten million lire for that tower, not one million which is what he claimed. Ada would give you fifteen for it. You should make a decision.

I think you'll need shirts and socks, and maybe a dark jacket. I can't possibly take care of that for you as I am sick, and Angelica doesn't have time. Viola is rather down, depressed, I think she had a minor nervous breakdown. We're all in a bad way. Matilde has completely lost her mind over *Polenta and Poison*. She goes to see Colarosa, the editor, every day to read proofs or look at the cover, or just to break his spirit. Your friend, Mara Martorelli, is working there now. Matilde saw her. She says that she was wearing a wild Japanese kimono covered with giant flowers.

I'm ending this letter here because Angelica is waiting for me so she can mail it.

I'm sending you hugs and wish you happiness, if there is such a thing as happiness. A possibility that we can't entirely exclude, despite so rarely seeing evidence of it in this world that's been given to us.

Your mother

22

February 29, 1971

Dear Michele,

I received the twelve onesies. You shouldn't have bothered sending them as they are very worn out, the snaps are torn, and the fabric is stiff and scratchy like salt cod. Tell your Eileen, or whatever her name is, that I'm not a pauper. Tell her that my baby's onesies are new and soft. They are made of beautiful pink and blue flowered material. Nevertheless, thank you anyway.

I hereby announce that I have moved in with the pelican. I got here two nights ago after that friend of mine told me to pack up my stuff and move out of Via dei Prefetti. I had told her about the pelican and she said so I didn't need the place on Via dei Prefetti anymore and so I should leave. She has this idea about turning the apartment into a club or art gallery or something. She's not planning to make it a boutique anymore. Either way, she told me, she needed a lot of money and that I should leave and not give her any trouble about it. Of course I could have argued the point and stayed longer but I got angry and in twenty minutes I was packed up, had the baby, loaded everything into the stroller, and headed over to Fabio's place. Fabio, the pelican. He has a loft in Piazza Campitelli. It's a wonderful apartment and I don't have the long commute from Via dei

Prefetti anymore. He was quite surprised to see me there in the middle of the night but immediately sent the maid to buy milk for the baby and some chicken for me at Piccione, that cafe on Largo Argentina. The baby is drinking regular milk now. I can't remember if I told you. No more formula.

I'd been to Fabio's before and I like his loft a lot. The only thing I don't like is his cleaning woman. She's fiftyish and big and tall and has a hard, unkind face. She looks at me so harshly and doesn't respond when I address her. She acts like the baby is a dirty rag that's in her way. I suggested to Fabio that he fire her, and he thought about it but said she was irreplaceable.

I don't go to the office anymore. I stay home and enjoy the loft. I go out onto the terrace and tan. I take the baby out with me and keep him under the umbrella. I can't tell you how great it is for both of us. I don't have to leave the baby with that woman anymore. She ignored him and didn't change his diapers and I'm sure she just let him cry. When he gets back from work, Fabio comes out onto the terrace too and we hold hands and Belinda brings us tomato juice. Belinda is the fifty-year-old in the pink apron. When I ask him if he's happy now, he wrinkles his big nose and says he is. The relationship with Ada is over. He doesn't see her anymore. I phoned Osvaldo to find out how Ada took the news. He said she took it badly but predicted that my relationship with the pelican won't last long. But I think I'll marry the pelican. I will have more children because I like having children more than anything else in the world. Of course, you need money to have children, otherwise it's horrible, but I figured out that the pelican is a millionaire. I'm not going to marry him for money. I'm marrying him because I love him, but I am happy about all the money. I'm envious about how rich he is, and how smart, and sometimes I even feel as if I envy his enormous nose.

I send you huge congratulations on your wedding and you should send me some for mine because you'll see I might even get married before you do.

I'm giving you a painting by Mario Mafai for your wedding. I'm not sending it to you because it's not a simple matter to send a Mario Mafai painting. It's hanging in the bedroom here in the pelican's house and I asked him if I could give it to you and he said yes.

Mara

23

March 18, 1971—Leeds

Dear Angelica,

I received the papers, thank you. I got married on Wednesday.

I'm sorry to hear Mamma is sick. I hope it's nothing too serious.

Eileen and I found a small two-story house on "Nelson Road," which is an endless street and all the houses are identical. We have two square meters of garden in which I will plant roses.

I want to thank Mamma for the money, shirts, and the dark suit, which I didn't wear on my wedding day. I'll never wear it. I put it away in the closet with some mothballs.

Eileen goes to the university early in the morning and brings the children to school. I go out a little later. I clean the house, wash the dishes, and vacuum. At least this has been the schedule for the last two days. All is well.

On my wedding day, we had dinner in a restaurant with Eileen's parents. Eileen's parents are in love with me.

I heard that Viola and Elio wanted to come to my wedding. I heard it from Signora Peroni's cousin, who came to stay in the same boardinghouse where I was living until the day before yesterday. Luckily they didn't come, luckily none of you did. It's not that I don't want to see you. I'd be so happy to see everyone, but we did the wedding ceremony quickly, and we didn't worry about the sorts of things that you, Viola, Elio, or any of you would have, and you would have been disappointed if you'd been there.

Tell Oreste that my wife is a member of the Communist party, she's one of very few Communists around here. I'm still not a Communist. I'm still not anything and I lost contact with those friends I had in Rome and haven't heard anything more about them. To think, I actually left for political reasons. Well, not just for political reasons. It's not that easy to explain why I left. Anyway, I don't think about politics now. I think about my wife, and that's enough for me.

I need a book, Kant's *Critique of Pure Reason*. See if you can find it in my studio, if my studio is still there, and if I can still call it mine.

Michele
Ti abbraccio

24

March 23, 1971

Dear Michele,

I'm back on my feet, it's been two days and I'm feeling better, I'm still run down but that will pass.

A letter from you would have meant a great deal to me, but you're so stingy about writing to your mother. I heard the news anyway, through Angelica. I'm glad you have a nice house, at least I imagine it's nice, with a little garden and a carpet you vacuum. I can't imagine you vacuuming. I can't even imagine you planting roses. The idea of planting roses right now seems so foreign to me, I wonder if I'd even know how, and yet that's one of the reasons I moved to the country. It might be because it's still winter, and still cold, and it rains all the time, but I have the impression that I won't be planting a garden even once spring has arrived, I'll probably call a gardener and won't touch a leaf myself. I don't have a green thumb, though apparently Ada does. Roses in particular remind me of the Via dei Villini house, where we had that beautiful rose trellis right under my window. It wasn't even our garden, it belonged to the neighbors. In the end, roses remind me of Filippo. Not that I want to forget him, there are hundreds of memories, the paths in my mind that lead to him are too many, but I must have been looking at those roses when he told me it was over and so now whenever I see a rose trellis, I feel like I've suddenly fallen into darkness, and so while I hope there will be flowers in my new garden, there won't be roses.

Since you and I are similar in so many ways, I don't believe you're capable of tending to flowers. But then it's possible that you've changed in these last months and are a different person from the one I knew and different from me. It's possible that Eileen has changed you more. I have confidence in Eileen. I think I'll like her. Would you send me a picture of her? The one you sent is so small, all I can make out is a long raincoat. You've also said that she's very intelligent. I'm like you, I love intelligence. I always try to surround myself with intelligent people. Your father was peculiar and brilliant. We were able to live together because we both had such strong personalities and both of us needed a lot of space. Filippo is peculiar and very smart. Sadly, he left me. He is completely gone from my life. We never see each other anymore. We could have remained friends if that was what I'd wanted, but I didn't. Anyway, we would have had to see each other in the presence of that harried-looking woman he married. She must be utterly stupid. Maybe our relationship wore him out. I don't think I'm very intelligent but I might have been too intelligent for him. Not everyone loves intelligence. I have such wonderful memories of my years with Filippo, even though it all ends in this darkness. The memories are marvelous. He never wanted to live together, he always had so many excuses ... his studies, it would have upset the twins, his health, the health of his mother. They were all excuses, though. To be frank, he didn't want to live with me. Maybe he didn't love me enough. But I do have good memories of the hours spent with Filippo in the Via dei Villini house. He played chess with Viola and Angelica and helped them with their homework, made curried rice, used the typewriter in my room to work on the draft of *Religion and Pain*. I thought a lot about Filippo during my illness, I even wrote him a letter and then tore it up. He had a baby girl just a few days ago. They sent me an announcement with a picture of a flying pink swan on it. What stupidity. They named the baby Vanessa. Stupidity. You tell me, what kind of name is that for a baby girl.

I'm writing you from my room, there's a fire in the fireplace. I can see our bare garden through the window, it's flat, there are no flowers, just the wrought iron lamp posts, the fake carriage, I chose it all without really believing in it. Those two dwarf spruces that Matilde picked out and that I hate. I can see the village in the distance, and the moon over the hills. I'm wearing a black dress that I think suits me and when I go down to dinner I'll put on that Spanish scarf that your father gave me maybe twenty years ago, it was in a chest with mothballs and I pulled it out. Osvaldo and Colarosa, the editor, are coming to dinner. Matilde invited Colarosa. He's earned a dinner invitation, Matilde has broken his spirit in every possible way. You should know that *Polenta and Poison* finally came out. We have copies all over the house. Matilde sent you an inscribed copy. You'll see the hills, the sun, and the fields. Matilde drew the cover. Colarosa suggested using a Van Gogh painting on the cover, but there was no reasoning with her. When Matilde gets an idea in her head about something, nothing will change her mind. Everyone told her the cover looked like socialist propaganda. But she could not be convinced.

Matilde went to Rome yesterday to buy champagne for to-night. She planned the whole menu herself and has spent the day in the kitchen getting on Cloti's nerves. Cloti is already in such a fury and nervous enough as it is. We are having a rice timbale, vol-au-vent with chicken and béchamel sauce, and sponge cake. I pointed out to Matilde that all the food is round. I also pointed out that all those dishes are quite heavy. A dinner like that could kill a bull.

Matilde wants the twins to put on lace-collared velvet dresses and wear their hair out. She's going to wear a Cossack blouse and her black skirt. I haven't met Colarosa yet. Matilde tells me he's short, his head sits right on his shoulders, and that he has a remarkable nose. I'd wanted to invite Ada too but Osvaldo explained that Ada and Colarosa, the editor, were lovers and now they're broken up. He's with your friend Mara Castorelli now. She descended on him late one night, the baby in her arms. To think that Ada got her that job and Mara stole him away as fast as lightning. I don't know if Mara will be coming tonight too, I said she could, of course, but it seems as if she doesn't know what to do with the baby. I'll have Ada over another time. I haven't met her yet and she's been unspeakably kind to me. She's the reason they're going to install a telephone here. I can hardly believe that I'm going to have a telephone here. I'm going to call you first thing. Even though the idea of calling you makes me nervous. I don't think I'll have the nerve, my heart isn't strong enough. I was such a bull once. But now so much has happened. I'm fragile.

I hear a car. They have arrived. I must leave you now.

Your mother

I just saw a small figure in a mink coat climb out of the car. It must be Mara.

March 26, 1971

Dear Michele,

I had dinner at your mother's house a few nights ago. It was not fun. Osvaldo and Angelica were there, and the pelican, your aunt, your mother, and your little sisters. I don't know why I wanted to meet your mother and wanted her to like me. Maybe because I was hoping that she'd help me get you to marry me. To be clear, I've never wanted to marry you. Or at least I never thought that's what I wanted. But maybe out of desperation I wanted that without knowing that I did.

I wore a long black and silver dress that the pelican had bought for me that same afternoon. And a mink coat that the pelican also bought for me five days ago. I kept the coat on all night because your mother's house is so damn cold. The thermostat is defective. Wearing that dress and coat made me feel legitimate, I can't explain why. It made me feel sweet, and ever so small. I wanted everyone to look at me and think how sweet and small I am. I wanted this so badly that when my voice came out of my mouth it was sweet and gentle. And then, at a certain point, the thought occurred to me, "These people probably all think that I'm just a high-class call girl." The phrase, high-class call girl, is something I'd read in a mystery novel that morning. As soon as I thought up those words I could feel them falling down on me like stones. It made me think that everyone was being standoffish with me. Even Osvaldo. Even Angelica. Even the pelican. The pelican spent the whole evening curled into a corner of the couch with a glass in his hand. He stroked his hair. He stroked his nose. He didn't wrinkle his nose, he smoothed it down, slowly. Your mother is beautiful, but I'm not sure she's very nice. She was wearing a black dress and a fringed scarf that she kept fiddling with, and she fiddled with her hair which is exactly like yours, curly and auburn. I thought to myself that if you'd been in the room, it would have been easier for me, because you are perfectly aware that I'm not a slut, high or low class, you know I'm just a girl. There was a fire in the fireplace and I was still cold.

Your mother asked me where I was from and I told her Novi Ligure. I started making up all sorts of things about Novi Ligure. I said that I have a big gorgeous house there and lots of adoring relatives waiting for me, a dear old nanny, and a wonderful little brother. In fact, the dear old nanny is an old lady who cooks for my cousins. I do love my brother but I never write him. My cousins' house is nothing special as houses go. It's on top of a store. A crockery store. My cousins sell crockery. I didn't tell them that. I told them that they were all lawyers.

Your mother and Angelica were busy in the kitchen because your mother's housekeeper suddenly got sick and had to go to bed. The truth is, she was offended by something your aunt had said about her vol-au-vent. That's what Angelica told me. Your little sisters refused to help because they said they were too tired, and played ping-pong instead. They were still wearing their gym clothes and refused to change and that made your aunt angry too. That, on top of the vol-au-vent being all mushy and liquid inside.

I started getting depressed at a certain point. I thought, What am I doing here? Where am I? Why am I wearing a fur coat? Who are these people who don't ask me practically anything and can't seem to hear me when I speak? I told your mother that I wanted to bring my baby over to meet her. She said I could but didn't seem enthusiastic about it. I was dying to start screaming about how the baby was yours. If I was a hundred percent sure I would have. There were pictures of you from when you were little, they were everywhere, and when I looked at them I realized that my baby does look like you, around the mouth and chin. But it's hard to be sure. Similarities aren't proof of anything.

They didn't talk a lot but I couldn't understand much of what they said. They are intellectuals. I was dying to start shouting at them that as far as I was concerned they were all big assholes. I didn't even like Angelica. I didn't understand anyone. The pelican was very serious there. He didn't even look at me. Every so often, I'd try to hold his hand and he'd pull it away. I got the impression that I was annoying him every time I spoke. He had never been with me with other people and maybe he was ashamed. At the end of dinner they poured champagne. I said, "I would like to congratulate you ever so much on *Polenta and Chestnuts*." I got the title wrong. The pelican corrected me. I said I had gotten confused because of the song that goes: *Non andare sulle montagne ... Mangerai polenta e castagne ... ti verrà acidità* ("don't go into the mountains ... they'll feed you corn and grits ... then you'll have indigestion"). I decided to sing the whole song. It's a cute song and I am tone-deaf. Your mother smiled a little. Osvaldo smiled a little. The pelican didn't smile at all. The twins didn't smile. You could feel the ice in the room while I was singing. Your aunt went out to knock on the housekeeper's door with a plate of vol-au-vent and other leftovers but came back mortified because the woman refused it all.

We drove home in Osvaldo's Fiat. Me, Angelica, and the pelican. I sat in the back with the pelican. I told him, "I don't know what your problem with me is. I don't know what I did to you. You didn't say a word to me all night. You didn't even look at me." He said, "I have a terrible headache." "My God, you always have a headache," I said, because he always has a headache. He was flattening himself into that back seat. As if he didn't want to touch me. So I started crying, quietly, not hard, and the tears were getting on my fur. Angelica rubbed my knee. Osvaldo was driving and didn't turn around. The pelican just shrank into his corner, wrapping his coat around him, his nose perfectly still. It was terrible to be crying in the middle of all that iciness. It was worse than singing. Much worse.

I'd left the baby at home with the maid, Belinda. I should have brought him along. Belinda has no patience with babies. The baby was crying when I walked in and Belinda was standing there waiting to leave. She told me that she had a right to a good night's sleep. I told her that I have a right to relax sometimes. She told me that I didn't have a right to anything. I didn't answer her at first. I slammed the door in her face. Then I yelled and told her that she was fired. I've already fired her a number of times. But she says she won't go. She says she needs to hear it from the professor himself. The professor is the pelican.

The baby cried all night long. It was awful. Poor child, he's teething. I walked him back and forth in the living room, tears streaming down my face. It was almost morning before he fell asleep. I put him in the stroller. I felt sorry for him because he was so tired of crying, he was sweaty, puffy, his hair was wet and clinging to his head, he slept like a rag. I felt sorry for myself because I was dead tired and still wearing the silver and black dress. I hadn't had time to change. I went into the bedroom. The pelican was awake, lying there with his arms crossed behind his head. I was annoyed at all of it. His pajamas, his head on the pillow, his nose, were all annoying. I said to him, "I don't think I can go on like this. We need to hire a nanny." "A nanny?" he said, as if he'd fallen from the moon. "When I lived alone," I said, "at Via dei Prefetti, when the baby was really bad I could let him cry a little but I can't do that here because of your headaches." "I don't think I could have a nanny here too," he said. "I don't think that I want that at all, not at all." "So I should just go back to living alone," I said. He didn't answer. We stayed like that, lying down, not moving, on ice like two dead people.

In a previous letter, I told you that me and the pelican were going to get married. That was a dumb idea. Pretend I never said that. Tear that letter up, because I'm ashamed of having said it. He never dreamed of marrying me and maybe I never wanted to marry him either.

He's gone now. Before he went out the door, I yelled, "And you can stop treating me like a high-class call girl!" There was no soft voice left in me, that voice I had when I felt good and small. This harsh sound came out of my mouth, like a land-lady's. He didn't answer me.

He left.

There are times that I get furious. I think to myself: I'm so pretty, charming, so young and good, and I have such a handsome baby. I do this person the great favor of living with him in his house and spending the money that he doesn't need. But what does this asshole want from me in the end. Sometimes I'm so angry, that's what I think.

Mara

26

March 29, 1971—Novi

Dear Angelica,

You'll be surprised to hear that I'm writing you from Novi Ligure. I arrived yesterday. I'm here with the baby at the house of my cousin's maid. She put a mattress down in the kitchen for me. She's old. Her name is Amelia. She said I can stay here for a few days, but not more than that because she doesn't have the space. I don't know where to go, but that's not important, because I always end up somewhere.

I left suddenly. I wrote Fabio a note. He wasn't home. I wrote, "I'm leaving. Thank you. Bye." I took the fur because it was a present and also because I was cold. And the silver and black dress that I wore to your mother's house. I took that too, it's not like he can use it. Anyway, they were presents.

I want to ask you a favor. In my rush to leave I forgot my kimono, the black one with the sunflowers. Can you get it and send it to me here in Novi Ligure, 6 Via Della Genovina. It should be in the dresser in our room in the bottom drawer. I realize that I wrote "our room" because it was "our room" for a time and we were so happy, me and him. If there is such a thing as happiness, that was it. Only it didn't last long. You see, happiness doesn't last long. Everyone knows that.

You might think it's weird to fall in love with a man like that, he isn't the least bit handsome and he has that big nose. A pelican. When I was little I had a book with pictures of all the animals, there was a pelican, with his giant red beak and short legs rooted to the ground. That's him. But you know you can fall in love with anyone, even absurd, weird, sad men. I liked how rich he was because all the money he had seemed different from all the money that other people have. It was as if his money stuck to him like the tail of a comet. I liked how intelligent he was, that he knew about so many things that I didn't. His mind seemed to stretch behind him like a comet tail too. I don't have a tail. I'm poor and stupid.

When I first met the pelican, I didn't think much of him, and I didn't think of him romantically at all. I thought, This guy here is going to swallow me up like a raw egg. And I'll spend all his money. I stole him from that ridiculous Ada. I set up myself and my baby in his house and that was that. I was cool, calm, and happy. Then this dreadful sadness started growing in me. He put all of his depression onto me, the same way you pass on a virus. I could feel it in my bones, even when I was sleeping. I couldn't free myself of it. But his depression made him smarter and I just got stupider. Because depression is different for everyone.

That's how I figured out I'd fallen into a trap. I was madly in love with him and he couldn't have cared less for me. He was bored of having me around. But he didn't have the courage to kick me out, because he felt bad. And he made me feel bad. Living in the middle of all those bad feelings was exhausting, exhausting for me and for him.

I'll bet that he was just as indifferent to Ada. Except that she's strong, lively, optimistic, and always has a million things to do.

She's not clingy at all. But I'm heavy and clingy. He would just sit there, lost in his misery and I could tell that I would never fit into this misery, there was never any room for me. The "never" scared me. So I left.

I frightened Amelia to death when I arrived last night. We haven't seen each other in three years and she doesn't know about anything that's happened. I never wrote her, not even a rotten postcard. She didn't know that I'd had a baby. She looked at me, the baby, the fur coat, and couldn't understand any of it. I told her I had a baby with a man who later turned me out onto the street. I asked her for a place to sleep. She pulled this mattress out of a wardrobe. I told her I was hungry and she made me dinner, a fried egg and a plate of beans. I figured she would let me stay because she felt sorry for me. That's how you get through life, making people feel sorry for each other.

During the day, Amelia cooks for my cousins. There are a lot of them and lots to cook. I asked her not to say anything about me to my relatives but she went and told them first thing that I was staying with her. And so all of a sudden two of my cousins and my brother show up, my twelve-year-old brother who lives with them and helps around the store. They love my brother. But he's not very affectionate. He's a cold fish. He wasn't surprised by the baby. He didn't act happy. Neither did my cousins. If I'd shown up with a cat they might have acted more excited. My fur coat was hanging over a chair and they were excited by that. They said I could live for years off what I'd get selling the coat. I could tell they were thinking about buying it from me themselves. But I told them I didn't have any intention of selling it at this point. I'm fond of my fur. I remember the day we went to buy it, me and the pelican, holding hands, when he was happy to walk down the street with me. Maybe back then he was already starting to think that I was a little clingy and too heavy. But I didn't know then he was thinking that.

If the pelican asks you for my address you can give it to him.

Mara

Ti abbraccio

27

April 2, 1971

Dear Mara,

Angelica came over to get your kimono. We looked for it for a long time because it wasn't in the dresser in the bedroom but had ended up in my office, under a stack of newspapers. It was dusty and I hesitated to ask Belinda to wash it, I didn't want to remind her of you. She erased every trace of your stay here the morning you left. She threw away the face cream in the bathroom and all the baby food. I told her that I liked to eat baby food but she told me that you bought a particularly bad quality baby food. Angelica shook out your kimono a little, beat it with her hands and said she could just send it like that.

I'm sending you money because I think you'll need it. Angelica is going over to San Silvestro to mail the kimono and wire money.

I am deeply grateful to you for leaving. In all honesty it was my most ardent desire and you understood that; perhaps because my behavior led you to want to leave. My words may seem uselessly cruel to you. They are in fact cruel but they are not useless. If you were to harbor deep down some dark, confused notion about coming back, you should extinguish those hopes entirely. I cannot live with you. I probably cannot live with anyone. My mistake was to fool myself and fool you into the idea that a long-term relationship between the two of us would be possible. Yet, I did not invite you, you are the one who came to me. Our already fragile union was shattered under the stress of trying to live together. Regardless, I share the blame and don't want to minimize my part. These grievances accumulate upon the ones I already have about life—a burden that is already too heavy. I feel great pity for you and was not brave enough to tell you to leave. You will say I'm criminal. Indeed, that word perfectly describes me. I feel great pity for you and also for myself, it is the tattered self-pity of a criminal. When I returned home the other night and you weren't there and then I read your note, I sat down on the couch and missed you. I felt such emptiness. In the middle of this feeling though there was a kind of giddiness and the most overwhelming relief, an ardent joy, nothing I should hide from you because it's right for you to know what I was feeling. In short, I could not stand you for another minute.

I wish you all the best opportunities for the future and I wish you happiness if there is such a thing as happiness. I don't believe there is, but other people do, and who am I to say they are wrong.

The Pelican

28

March 27, 1971—Leeds

Dear Angelica,

Mara wrote. Can you go visit and comfort her? She's got so many problems. That editor she's living with—apart from his dreadful error of judgment in having published *Polenta and Poison*—has infected her with all this sadness and confusion.

Maybe I can come during Easter vacation. I'm not sure. I miss my family sometimes, "my people," as they say, even though you're not at all *mine* as I am not at all *yours*. But if I were to come, you would all be watching me. Your eyes would be on me the whole time. Do I even need to add that you'd be watching my wife too because she'd be with me and you'd all try to figure out the nature of our relationship, how good it is. I couldn't bear that.

I also miss my friends a lot, Gianni, Anselmo, Oliviero, and the others. I don't have friends here. I even miss some parts of Rome. There are other parts and other friends who I miss but who I also find repulsive. When nostalgia and repulsion get mixed together then all the places and people we love from a distance seem to sit at the far end of a broken, impassable road.

Sometimes the nostalgia and repulsion are so intertwined in me that I can feel them when I'm sleeping, it wakes me up and I have to get out of bed and go smoke. Then Eileen takes her pillow to go sleep with the children. She says she has the right to her sleep. She says we each have to deal with our own nightmares. She's right. She's not wrong.

I don't know why I'm writing these things to you. But I'm in a place right now where I think I could sit and chat with a chair. I can't talk to Eileen because first of all, it's Saturday and she has to cook meals for the whole week. Second, because she doesn't really love listening. Eileen is very intelligent, but I've discovered that all her intelligence gives me nothing because it's reserved for things that have nothing at all to do with me, like nuclear physics. Deep down, I think I'd rather have a stupid wife who stupidly and patiently listens to me. Right now, I wouldn't mind having Mara around. I couldn't stand her in the long run, because she'd listen to me and then she'd dump all her problems on me and she'd stick to me like taffy and I'd never have a moment's peace ever again. I wouldn't want her as a wife, but in this particular moment, I wouldn't mind having her here with me.

Michele
Ti abbraccio

29

April 2, 1971

Dear Michele,

I just got your letter. It left me with an awful feeling. You're obviously very unhappy.

Maybe I shouldn't overdramatize your letter. Maybe I should tell myself that you had a little fight with your wife and you're feeling alone. But I can't help overdramatizing. I'm worried.

I could come to you if you're not coming here. It wouldn't be easy because I don't know what to do with my child, or Oreste, and plus I don't have any money, but that's the least of my concerns because I can get some from Mamma. Mamma isn't well, she keeps getting a slight fever and of course I'm not going to tell her that I got a letter from you that worried me. If I decide to come visit, I'll ask her for money. I'll just tell her you're not coming because of work and so I decided to go visit you myself.

You say that right now you don't want the eyes of the people who love you watching you. It is really difficult to bear the gaze of people who love you when you're having a hard time, but you can get over that. People who love you may be judgmental, but their vision is clear, merciful, and severe, and that can be rough, but it's just healthy to face clarity, severity, and mercy.

Your friend Mara has left Colarosa. She wrote me from Novi

Ligure where she is staying with her cousins' maid. She's not doing well, she doesn't have anywhere to live, and has nothing to call her own, except for a black kimono with sunflower embroidery, a fox-fur coat, and a baby. But I feel like all of us are vulnerable to the gentle art of ending up in terrible situations that are unresolvable and impossible to move out of either by going forward or back.

Just write back a single line to let me know if I should come. I don't want to if the idea strikes you as unbearable.

Angelica

30

April 5, 1971

Dear Angelica,

Don't come. Eileen has family coming in from Boston. We only have one guest room. We might all go to Bruges. I've never seen Bruges.

Also, I've never met these relatives. Sometimes it's easier to be with strangers.

Avoid forming hypotheses about me. Anything that you would hypothesize would be wrong because you don't have all the essential information.

I would have liked to see you but it will have to be another time.

Michele

31

April 8, 1971

Dear Michele,

I just got your letter. I'll confess that I'd already packed my bag to come to you. I didn't ask Mamma for money, I asked Osvaldo. Uncharacteristically, he had it and didn't have to run to Ada.

Your letter made me laugh, the phrase, "I've never seen Bruges" … as if Bruges was the only place in the world you hadn't seen.

I want to see you, not just to talk about you but also to talk about me. I'm going through some things too.

But, as you say, that will have to be for another time.

Angelica

32

April 9, 1971

Dear Michele,

Angelica told me you're not coming for Easter. I'll be patient. I can't even count the number of times I've had to be patient when it comes to you. With every passing year, one's store of patience inevitably grows. It's the only resource that grows. All the others tend to wither.

I had arranged the two rooms on the top floor for you. I made the beds and hung towels in the bathroom. The bathroom on the top floor is the loveliest in the whole house, with its green arabesque patterned tiles, and I was pleased to think your wife would see it. The rooms are still in perfect order, the beds are ready. I haven't gone back up there. I will tell Cloti to go up and unmake the beds.

While I was arranging the rooms, I kept thinking about how your wife would feel comfortable here and that she would think that I have a nice house. What a stupid thing to think because I don't know your wife. I don't know what makes her comfortable or if she's the sort of person who likes well-kept houses or people who keep them.

Angelica tells me that you're going to Bruges instead. I can't imagine why you're going to Bruges, but at this point I've had to stop asking myself why you ever go one place or another. I try to imagine myself in one place or another in your life, but sense at the same time that your life is different than what I imagine, so the stories I imagine for you have become hazier and less and less reliable.

When I'm feeling better I want to come with Angelica to visit you, if you'd like that. We wouldn't stay at your house because we wouldn't want to be a bother to your wife, who I think always has a lot to do. We'd stay in a hotel. I don't love traveling and I don't love hotels either. But I'd rather stay in a hotel than feel as if I were being a burden, taking up space in a small house, because one of the very few things I know about your life is that you live in a small house. I can't come now because I haven't completely recovered from the pleuritis, which is to say that I don't have pleurisy anymore but the doctor says I still have to take care of myself. He says my heart is in disrepair. Explain to your wife that I'm a person whose house is in order but whose heart is in disrepair. Tell her what I'm like so that when she meets me she can compare the real me to your description. That's one of the few pleasures life affords, comparing the way others describe you with your own fantasies and with reality.

I think of your wife often and try to imagine her, even if you haven't tried to describe her and the picture you sent when you wrote to say you were getting married is small and blurry. I look at it frequently but can't make out anything except a long, black raincoat and a head wrapped in a scarf.

You never write me, but I'm glad you write Angelica. I think it comes more naturally for you to write her because you're closer to her than to me. Maybe I'm being optimistic, but I like to think that when you confide in her you're secretly confiding in me too. Angelica is very intelligent. She might be the most intelligent of all of us, even though passing judgment on the intelligence of your own children is a tricky matter.

At times I get the impression that you're unhappy. But Angelica is secretive with me. I believe that her secretiveness doesn't stem from a lack of affection but because she doesn't want me to worry. It seems strange to say, Angelica is very maternal with me. When I ask her about herself, her answers feel manufactured, calm and cold. In other words, I don't know much about Angelica. When we're together we don't talk about her, we talk about me. I'm always willing to talk about myself because I'm very alone, but as I'm so alone I don't have much to report about myself. I mean, I don't have much to report about my daily life. My days are monotonous when I'm not feeling well. I don't go out much, I might take the car out, sit on the couch for hours, watch Matilde do her yoga. Matilde, the lone wolf, Matilde at the typewriter working on her new book, Matilde making herself a beret from leftover yarn.

Viola told me she's angry at you because you've never written her, not even a postcard. She bought you a beautiful silver vase for your wedding and wanted to give it to you when you came. Please write Viola and thank her for the beautiful vase. Write to the twins too, they've been waiting for you and have gifts for Eileen's children, a jackknife and a teepee. Of course, I wish you'd write me too.

Osvaldo left for Umbria yesterday with Elisabetta and Ada. So we won't have his evening visits for the next week. I've gotten used to having him show up in the evening. I've gotten used to seeing him for a few hours, his red face and his big head and tousled thinning hair. He must have gotten used to spending evenings in this house too, playing ping-pong with the twins and reading Proust aloud to me and Matilde. When he's not here he goes to see Angelica and Oreste, where he does the same sorts of things but slightly differently, for example, he'll read Paperino to the baby and play tombola with Oreste and their friends, the Bettoias. Oreste finds him pleasant but useless. The Bettoias think he's useless but nice. One can't say that he isn't nice. I don't think useless is the right word, because a person can't have expectations from a useless person. Instead I expect that suddenly one day all the reasons for his existence on earth will be revealed to us. I think he's very intelligent, but he keeps his intelligence locked away in his chest, in his sweater, in his smile, keeping it hidden away for his own secret reasons. Even when he smiles I think he's a sad man. That may be why I've gotten so used to his company. I love sadness. I love sadness even more than intelligence.

You and Osvaldo were friends and I've so rarely had the pleasure of knowing one of your friends. I occasionally ask him about you. But his answers are mechanical, the same as Angelica's when I ask her how thing are going with her, whether she's happy. I get the impression that Osvaldo doesn't want to worry me either. Now that he's not here, I've come to detest that calmness and his elusive, harmless responses. But when he's here, I settle and accept his silence and his elusive responses. The years have made me resigned and docile.

The other day I was remembering that time you came over and the moment you arrived, you started going through all the dressers looking for a Sardinian tapestry that you wanted to hang on your wall in the workshop. That must have been the last time I saw you. I hadn't been in this house more than a few days. It was November. You went tearing through the rooms and upending dressers, everything that had just been put into place, and I followed you, complaining about how you always took my things. You must have found the tapestry because it's not here. It wasn't in the studio either. The tapestry doesn't mean very much to me, and it didn't mean anything to me back then. I think of it now perhaps because it's connected to the last time I saw you. I remember feeling a big sense of happiness in the middle of the arguing and my being angry at you. I knew that my nagging would irritate you but also make you happy. I remember it now as a happy day. It's unfortunate that we rarely recognize the happy moments while we're living them. We usually only recognize them with the distance of time. I was happy complaining about the way you were going through my dressers. But I have to say that you and I lost a precious day. We could have sat down and talked about incredibly important things. That might have made us less happy, it may have even made us unhappy. Now I'm going to remember that day, not as a vaguely happy day, but as a day of essential truth for both of us, destined to illuminate your being and my being, the way we always speak with modest words, we never use clear and urgent words, our words are gray, harmless, floating, and useless.

Ti abbraccio
Your mother

33

Dear Angelica,

I am friends with Michele and Eileen. I met Michele at the film society. He had me over to dinner several times and that's how I met Eileen.

I am Italian and am here in Leeds on a fellowship.

I got your address from Michele. He told me to visit you if I was back in Italy over the summer.

I'm writing to let you know that your brother has left his wife and we don't know where he's ended up. His wife isn't writing herself because she barely knows Italian and because she is in very bad shape. I feel quite sorry for her even though I don't want to judge Michele. I also felt sorry for him when I saw him in the squalid hotel when he left.

Eileen wanted me to tell you that Michele left, first of all because she doesn't know if he told you about their marriage falling apart, and second because Michele didn't leave a forwarding address and he left behind some debt. She has no intention of paying it off and is hoping you will take care of it. He owes three hundred pounds. Eileen is wondering whether you could send her the three hundred pounds right away if possible.

Ermanno Giustiniani
4 Lincoln Road, Leeds

34

May 3, 1971

Dear Ermanno Giustiniani,

Tell Eileen that we will be sending the money through Lillino Borghi, a relative, who will be coming to England in the next few days.

In the meantime, if you find out where Michele is, I would be grateful if you could send me his address as soon as possible. We haven't heard anything from him. He'd written to me that he wanted to go to Bruges, but I don't know whether he ended up going there or somewhere else.

He had told me that he didn't have any friends in Leeds, but that might have been before he met you. Or else he lied, as he has perhaps lied about various other matters, and between his reticence and apparent lies, it's difficult for me to figure out his life. But I certainly don't judge him, and wouldn't in any case have any of the essential information with which to judge him. I can be upset about the lies and his evasiveness but there are unfortunate circumstances that lead some people to tell lies and be evasive, even if they don't want to be.

I'm not writing Eileen directly because I don't know English very well and also because I don't know what I'd say to her beyond expressing grief for what happened between them, but maybe you can pass that on to her for me.

Angelica Vivanti de Righi

35

May 15, 1971—Trapani

Dear Michele,

Don't be shocked, I'm writing to you from Trapani. I ended up in Trapani. I don't remember if I told you about the nice woman I became friends with when I was staying in that boardinghouse in Piazza Annibaliano, the Pensione Piave. At the time she said that I could come with the baby to stay with her in Trapani. Then I completely lost track of her and couldn't remember her last name, just her first. It's Lillia. She's fat and has all this curly hair. When I was in Novi Ligure, I wrote to a maid at the Pensione Piave, who I also only knew by her first name, Vincenza. I described the fat lady with the curls and the little baby. The maid sent me the address in Trapani, where the curly-haired lady's husband had opened a restaurant. I wrote her but didn't wait to hear back before setting off. So here I am. The husband wasn't at all happy to see me but the curly-haired lady said I was going to be a help around the house. I wake up at seven and bring her coffee, she's still in bed, in her dressing gown. Then I take care of both our babies. I go down to do shopping, clean the house, and make the beds. The curly-haired lady brings up something to eat from the restaurant, usually lasagna because she likes it so much. I don't really care for lasagna, or restaurant leftovers in general. The curly-haired lady is unhappy here. I think it's a squalid city. And the restaurant isn't doing very well. They have bills to pay. I offered to do the bookkeeping but the husband says that I don't seem suited for it and I think he's right. The curly-haired lady cries on my shoulder all the time. I'm not very good at consoling her because I'm unhappy too. But the baby loves it here. I take him and the other baby to the park in the afternoon. The curly-haired lady has a stroller that fits two babies. I chat with people I meet in the park and tell them lies. It's nice to talk to strangers when you're depressed. At least you can make things up.

Now the curly-haired lady isn't a stranger anymore. I know her face by memory and I know all her clothes, her underwear, the curlers she puts in at night to get all those curls. I watch her eat lasagna every day and get tomato sauce all over her mouth. I'm not a stranger to her either. Sometimes she treats me badly and I'll answer her rudely. I don't tell her lies anymore because I've already told her the whole truth while weeping on her shoulder. I told her that I don't have anyone and that everywhere I go I get kicked in the ass.

Her baby is seven months old and weighs nine kilograms, mine only weighs seven. But a pediatrician in Novi Ligure told me that it's not necessarily better for babies to be too fat. Other than that, my baby is rosier and more handsome, and I have to say that his hair has grown thick and blond, and it's not as red as yours and his eyes aren't exactly green, they're more gray with some green. There are moments when he's laughing that I think he looks like you, but he doesn't look like you at all when he's sleeping, he looks like my grandfather, Gustavo. The curly-haired lady says there's a blood test that will tell me if he's yours, but even that isn't totally certain. There's no sure way to find out if the baby belongs to someone else. What does it matter? In the end, I don't care and neither do you. The onesies your wife sent me would have come in handy now. I didn't appreciate them then but it turns out they're useful and sometimes I put the baby in one of the curly-haired lady's onesies when there's nothing else around.

I'm practically a servant here. I don't like being a servant. I doubt anyone likes it. I'm dead tired at night and my feet hurt. My room is off the kitchen. You could die of heat in there. They don't pay me at all, they say we have an even exchange. They slip me cash sometimes, when they think of it, but that's only happened twice since I got here. It is true though that they're in bad shape themselves.

I packed my fur in a dress bag and put it in the curly-haired lady's wardrobe. Every now and then she unzips it a little and strokes the sleeve. She says she wants to buy it but I don't want to sell it to her because I'm worried she won't be able to pay me enough, probably nothing at all. I had considered keeping it as a souvenir of the time I spent living with the pelican, but I'm going to sell it after all because I'm not sentimental like that. Occasionally I'll have a wave of sentimentality but it disappears instantly. I go back to being exactly who I am, not sentimental, a person with her feet planted solidly on the ground. Osvaldo says that I don't have my feet planted on the ground and that I gallop through the clouds and that might be true because I've really fallen hard some of these times.

I saw Osvaldo in mid-April when I stopped in Rome on my way here. I went to his shop and saw Signora Peroni, who was so happy to see me and the baby again. Then Osvaldo arrived. I asked after you but he didn't have any news and had just returned from his trip in Umbria with Ada, naturally. He took me to the station in his Fiat 500. He told me that the pelican had moved to one of his villas in Chianti and he's thinking about shutting down the publishing house because he's lost interest in it. Ada visited him in Chianti. But I don't care about the pelican anymore and the period of being a tearful wreck over him is done and it already seems so far in the past. What's important is to keep moving and avoid things that make you cry. Osvaldo told me I wouldn't be happy in Trapani and that they'd put me to work as a servant, which is exactly what has happened. But I told him that eventually, with patience, I would find another situation, maybe doing something like the work I was doing for the pelican before he dragged me away to go live in his penthouse. Though he didn't really drag me, I'm the one who showed up on his doorstep. Either way, Osvaldo didn't have any other suggestions, just that I shouldn't go to Trapani. Brilliant idea. I knew from the start that this city would kill me. It's so depressing at night. But you have to avoid looking out the window, jump right into bed, and pull the sheets up over your head.

Osvaldo waited with me until the train left. He sat in the compartment. He bought me magazines and sandwiches. He gave me money. I gave him my address in Trapani in case he gets it into his head to visit me. Then we hugged and kissed and while I was kissing him I realized that he's entirely queer. I had my doubts before but in that moment on the train, all my doubts disappeared.

I'll put my address at the bottom of this letter. I don't know if I'll stay here much longer, because now and then the curly-haired lady says they can't possibly afford a live-in maid. Sometimes she says that, and other times she hugs me and tells me that I'm great company. I feel sorry for the curly-haired lady. At the same time, I hate her. I have come to realize that the more you know someone the more you feel sorry for them. That's why strangers are better. Because you haven't started feeling sorry for them or hating them. I think I might die of the heat here in August. I'm in my room now. There's a window but you have to climb onto the bed in order to open it. It's already hot. The restaurant is below us, which makes it feel even hotter. I'm sitting on my bed as I write you and there's a pile of ironing beside me. Imagine, me starting to iron now.

I'm writing to you at your same Leeds address. I often wonder what kind of life you lead with your wife in that English city. Your life has to be better than what's become of mine. I haven't seen any men I like around here. Where are all the men I might like who might like me back? I wonder that sometimes.

Ti abbraccio

Mara

Via Garibaldi, 14—Trapani

36

June 4, 1971

Dear Mara,

I'm writing with difficult news. My brother Michele died during a student protest in Bruges. The police came to break up the crowd. He was chased by a gang of fascists and one of them stabbed him. They might have recognized him from somewhere. It was an empty street. Michele was with a friend who went to call an ambulance. During that time Michele was left alone on the sidewalk. The street had a lot of stores but they were all closed because it was ten at night. Michele died in the emergency room of the hospital at eleven. The friend telephoned my sister, Angelica. My sister and her husband and Osvaldo Ventura went to Bruges. They brought him back to Italy. We buried Michele yesterday in Rome next to our father who died last December, as you may remember.

Osvaldo told me to write you. He's too upset. I am upset too as you can imagine, but I'm trying to be strong. The news was in all the newspapers but Osvaldo says of course you don't read newspapers.

I know you loved my brother. I know that you wrote each other. You and I met once, at a party last year for Michele's birthday. I remember you well. We thought you should know of our terrible loss.

Viola

37

June 12, 1971

Dear Mara,

I know Viola wrote you. My daughter and I are staying at my mother's house now. I am keeping her company, we are spending these motionless days together, the days that come after a tragedy. Motionless ... even though there is so much to do, letters to write, photographs to look at, and silence, even though we try to talk as much as we can, tend to daily life. I guess we're gathering memories, distant memories, the ones that seem innocuous. Sometimes we get lost in small details and find ourselves talking out loud, and laughing hard, just to make sure we still have the ability to think about the present, the ability to talk out loud, and to laugh hard. But the instant we stop talking we can feel the silence. Osvaldo has come a few times. His visits don't disrupt the silence or the motionlessness and so they are comforting.

I was wondering whether you'd had any recent letters from Michele. He stopped writing to us. They still haven't found the people who killed him and we only have vague and confused information from the boy who saw it happen. I think Michele had gotten involved with politics again in Bruges and that the

141

people who killed him had some motive. But I'm just speculating. In reality we don't know anything and the only thing we can know is all speculation, which we go over and over, questioning ourselves, but we will never have a clear answer.

There are things I can't think about and mostly I can't think about the minutes Michele was alone on the street. I can't think that he was dying while I was at home, peacefully doing the same things I do every evening, washing dishes, washing Flora's tights, hanging them to dry on the balcony, until the phone rang. I can't think about everything I did that day because everything moves so steadily toward the ringing telephone. Michele had gained consciousness for a moment and gave that boy my number but then he died right afterward, which is terrifying, my telephone number is what came into his mind as he was dying. I couldn't understand what they were saying on the phone because they were speaking German. I don't know German. I called Oreste over because he speaks German. Oreste did everything after that. He took the baby to the Bettoias (our friends), he called Osvaldo and Viola, and Viola went over to tell my mother. I wanted to be the one to tell her, but I also needed to leave, and in the end I decided to leave because I wanted to say goodbye to Michele, to see those red curls of his one last time.

We said goodbye to him in the hospital chapel. Then we went to the place he'd been staying and they brought us his suitcase, coat, and red sweater. It was all on a chair in his room. He was wearing jeans and a white cotton button-down with a tiger's head on it. We had seen the shirt and jeans at the police station, they were bloodstained. The suitcase just had some underwear, a crumpled pack of cookies, and a train schedule. We went to see where he'd been killed. It was a narrow street with cement loading docks on both sides. At that time of day it was filled with the sounds of trucks. We were with his friend who'd been with him when he died. A Danish boy, seventeen years old. He took us to the sandwich shop where he and Michele had eaten that morning and the movie theater where they'd spent the afternoon. He had known Michele for three days. He couldn't tell us about Michele's other friends or who he'd been there with. So all we know about his time in that city is a boardinghouse, a sandwich shop, and a movie theater.

Write to me, send me news of you and the baby. I think about your baby now and then because Michele told me that it might have been his. I didn't think there was a resemblance when I saw him, but that doesn't mean it's not possible. Either way, I think we should care about your baby and not worry about whether or not it's his baby, by us I mean me and my mother and sisters, and I don't know why I feel that way, but not everything a person feels has to have an explanation, and to be perfectly honest I don't believe that obligations should have explanations. I think we will send you money periodically. Not that money will solve anything, since you're alone, broke, unsettled, and unreliable. But we're all unreliable and broken somewhere inside and sometimes it seems desperately attractive to be unrooted and breathing nothing but your own solitude. That's how people find each other, and understand.

Angelica

38

June 18, 1971—Trapani

Dear Miss Angelica,

I am a friend of Mara's. I'm writing you because Mara is too distraught to write you herself. Mara asked me to convey to you her condolences for the terrible misfortune that has befallen your family and I join her to convey my heartfelt condolences as well. Mara is so upset by this event that she hasn't eaten in two days. It is understandable as your dearly departed brother Michele was the father of Paolo Michele, the sweet angel, the adorable creature, who is at this moment amusing himself out on the balcony in the playpen, along with my own angel. I am writing you now in the name of these innocent souls, to plead with you not to forget Mara, who is currently helping me with small household tasks. I don't think I can keep her and her little angel with me here much longer. They are not a minor economic burden and even though I think of Mara like a sister, I actually do need real domestic help and Mara has too many problems to dedicate herself to housework, which requires patience, constancy, and goodwill. But neither I nor my husband have the heart to turn her out onto the street. I'm begging you to open your house to this innocent orphan of your own loved one taken too soon to heaven. I have more trouble, worries, and money problems than I can say. I did a good deed taking her in but I don't want to deprive others of the opportunity to do their duty and their own good deed.

I send greetings and devoted esteem, faithful that my pleas will be answered.

Lillia Savio Lavia

I also might permit myself to remind you that by taking in Mara you will have the great consolation of seeing the features of your loved one mirrored in the face of her sweet angel and such consolation gives comfort, a healing balm for the unrelenting grief of prostrate hearts.

39

Dear Angelica,

I'm in Varese now with Osvaldo's uncle. Osvaldo will have told you that the curly-haired lady and her husband put me out onto the street. I am so grateful for the money you sent, but unfortunately, I had to give almost all of it to the curly-haired lady because she said I broke an entire set of plates and that's actually the truth. I bumped into the table with the stroller one day when they had a dozen relatives over and all the plates went crashing to the ground.

When I found out about Michele's death I threw myself onto the bed to cry and stayed there all day, the curly-haired lady brought me broth because she's not mean when she's not worrying about cleaning the house or wasting money. Then, for the love of my baby I starting living again like before, and the curly-haired lady gave me vitamin shots because I was a wreck.

I didn't let the curly-haired lady read that letter from you, I kept all my letters hidden from her in a pair of boots, but I went into my room one day and found her standing by my dresser. She turned red and told me that she was looking for the plant sprayer and I told her that it was obvious she was going through my things and then we fought and it was the first time that we ended up screaming and yelling and I tore the sleeve off her dressing gown. We had another screaming and yelling fight the day that your wire came through but I knew there was nothing I could do and so I cashed the wire and threw the money in her face and she took it. That was just a few days before I left. Unfortunately I've come to understand that in my life, all my relationships fall apart eventually. I don't know if it's my fault or other people's, but my relationship with the curly-haired lady fell apart, and even though I know I should be grateful to her, I can't think of her with any affection or without getting upset.

It was very good of you to send money and I hope you'll thank your mother as well because I think it must have come from her. If you want to send money, know that I will always take it and be grateful, but to be honest, I need you to know that I don't think my baby is Michele's. He doesn't look like him. At times, he looks like my grandfather, Gustavo. But other times he looks like Oliviero, that boy who Michele was with a lot, the one who always wore that gray sweater that had two rows of little green trees running across it. I don't know if you remember Oliviero. I went out with him three or four times. I didn't like him at all, but it could have been him. What you said in your letter was so right, the part about me being broken and unreliable, but that you still understand me. I am so broken and unreliable, but I wanted you to know the truth because I don't want to deceive you. I guess I'm inclined to deceive everyone else but I don't want to deceive you. You said it so well: we don't need reasons for what we feel we need to do or not do. There aren't reasons. It would be a huge drag if there were reasons for everything.

I should continue my tale of disaster. The curly-haired lady and her husband went on a trip to Catania. They were supposed to be away for three days but their car broke down so they came home early and found me and one of their relations in their bed at three in the afternoon, on a Sunday.

The relation was actually his brother, and her cousin. He was eighteen. I say "was eighteen" because I haven't seen him since. He was over for lunch when I broke all the plates. He helped me sweep up and throw the shards away. It was Sunday and I was alone in the house, because they had, as I said, already left for Catania. I was putting the babies down for their afternoon nap. It was incredibly hot. All at once Peppino was standing in front of me. He had keys to the house but I hadn't heard the key in the lock and he frightened me. He was a tall boy with thick black hair. He'd been interested in me since the day of the broken plates. He looks a little like Oliviero. I closed the blinds in the children's room and we went into the kitchen. He told me he was hungry and wanted pasta. I had no desire to cook so I gave him a plate of lasagna. He said that he hated cold lasagna from the restaurant because he knew how they made it, they reused frying oil from a bottle and sauce made from leftover meat scraps on people's plates. We started gossiping about the restaurant and that led to us talking about the curly-haired lady and her husband, his brother. After all that gossiping we ended up in their bed, because my bed was tiny. I had showed it to him but he said the other bed was much better. We'd just finished having sex and were relaxing and cuddling, half asleep in the dim light when suddenly this curly head appeared in the doorway and then the big bald head and black glasses. Peppino pulled on his pants and undershirt right away and then grabbed for his button-down, I think he must have finished dressing in the stairwell because he rushed out of there fast, leaving me alone with those two snakes. They said I had to leave right away. I answered that I should wait for the babies to wake up from their nap but then both of them woke up and started crying. I went to pack my bag and in the meantime the curly-haired lady came in and suddenly started weeping on my shoulder and said that she understood, I was young, but her husband, he didn't understand and couldn't get over that I'd polluted their bed with his brother, and polluted the house, and the innocent children. The curly-haired lady had put milk for the baby in a plastic bottle. I asked her for a thermos but she didn't want to give me one because she only had one left, she'd given me her spare one when we were in the boarding-house. But I had lost it with all my moving around. The bottle she gave me must have been dirty because the milk went bad by nightfall and I had to throw it out. I told her I was leaving town and going to Rome but I didn't leave, I went to a bakery that I know. It was closed but I went around to ring at the back door. The baker told me I could spend the night in her house. Just one night, no longer. Then she made up a cot for me under the stairs and I set the baby up in my plastic suitcase but he got hot in there because he was used to the crib at the curly-haired lady's house. Later that night I tracked down Peppino, calling him at the restaurant, so he came to meet me and we went for a walk and then made love in a field near the train tracks. While we were having sex I thought to myself that I didn't care much about this Peppino because I never really liked younger men. I can only fall in love with older men who seem full of weird secrets and despair, like the pelican. But I have fun with younger men, and feel happy, and also sorry for them because they seem foolish and lost, like me, and I feel as if I'm alone but much happier. That was how it was with Michele. We had so much fun and the time we spent together was wonderful because it didn't have anything to do with true love but made me think of when I was little, playing ball with other children on our street. I was there with Peppino and all at once I started thinking about Michele and I wanted to cry and I thought that it would be a long time before I could feel happy again, if ever, because of all the things I know and remember. But Peppino thought I was crying because the curly-haired lady threw me out and he tried to comfort me in his own way, by pretending to be a cat, which he was very good at. But I kept weeping, thinking of Michele killed on the street and I said to myself that I was going to end up dead in the night on some street corner, nowhere near my baby, and that made me think of my baby who I'd left with the baker. I told Peppino to stop being a cat because it wasn't making me laugh anymore and then I remembered that I'd forgotten to pack my fur coat in all the chaos and it was still hanging in the curly-haired lady's suit bag. So the next day Peppino went to get it, using his key to sneak into the house, and then he brought it to me at the bakery. He didn't want to go back there because he was so scared of running into them on the stairway but I begged him. Eventually he agreed and he didn't run into anyone. I sold the fur to one of the baker's friends for four hundred thousand lire and then used that money to get myself a room in a motel. I called Osvaldo in Rome from the motel room and he said he would figure something out for me, and when he called back he said that I could go live in Varese with his uncle, an elderly gentleman who was looking for someone to sleep in his house so that he wouldn't be alone at night. And now here I am in a beautiful house with a garden full of hydrangea. I'm bored but happy and the baby is happy. Osvaldo's uncle is nice enough, he's handsome, he might be gay, he wears beautiful perfumed black velvet jackets. He doesn't do anything. He used to sell paintings and the house is full of them. But he's basically deaf as a post and he can't hear the baby crying at night. I have a gorgeous room with floral tapestries, it's nothing at all like that hole where I had to sleep in Trapani, and the most perfect thing about this place is that I don't have to do anything, except cut hydrangea for the vases and cook two soft-boiled eggs in the evening, one for the uncle and one for me. The only problem is that I might not be able to stay here because the uncle says that Ada is going to give him her maid and if she does that then he won't need me anymore. This Ada woman is always in my business. Otherwise I would stay here forever. I think I can tolerate boredom, though I get scared here in this lonely villa. I didn't used to be scared of anything but now I get scared and suddenly my throat tightens. I remember Michele and start thinking that I'm going to die too and that I might die here in this beautiful villa with the red carpet on the stairs and working faucets in all the bathrooms and vases of hydrangea everywhere, even in the kitchen, and pigeons cooing on the windowsill.

Mara

40

August 8, 1971

Dear Filippo,

I saw you yesterday in Piazza Spagna. I don't think you saw me. I was with Angelica and Flora. You were alone. Angelica said you looked older. I don't know if you look older. Your jacket was slung over your shoulders, your forehead was wrinkled the way it does when you walk. You were going to the tea room, Babington's.

It felt very strange to see you pass by on the street and not say hello. Though honestly, we wouldn't have had anything to say to each other. I don't care what's going on with you and you certainly don't care what's happening to me. What's going on with you means nothing to me because I'm unhappy. You don't care about what's going on with me because you are happy. Either way, you and I are strangers.

I know you went to the funeral. I wasn't there. Viola told me you had come. I know you told her you wanted to come by and visit me. You haven't yet. And I don't want to see you. In general, I don't want to see anyone except for my daughters and extended family, my sister-in-law Matilde, our friend Osvaldo Ventura. I can't say that I feel the desire for their company but if I don't see them for a few days, I miss them. It very well may be that if you came to see me a few times I'd get used to your visits. I don't want to get used to a presence that can't be depended on. That rosy maiden you married wouldn't let you come often. I would not be content with a lone, formal visit of condolence. That would do nothing for me.

It's also possible that in the period since we last saw each other you have become entirely stupid. I should clarify the term "rosy maiden." I'm not bitter. If I was once bitter or jealous, I have none of those feelings anymore, they've been decimated by the circumstances of my life.

I think of you every so often. This morning, out of the blue, I suddenly remembered the day you and I drove to Courmayeur in your car to visit Michele who was at camp. He was maybe twelve. I remember first seeing him standing there, shirtless and barefoot, in front of his tent. It made me so happy to see him like that, healthy, tan, the sprinkle of freckles, the ones he always had and then some extra ones. He used to get so pale in the city. He didn't go out much. His father didn't make him. The three of us had an excursion, we went to lunch in a chalet. You were nervous around Michele like you always were. You didn't love him. He didn't love you. You thought he was spoiled, presumptuous, capricious. He thought you were unfriendly. He never said it but it was clear to me that's what he thought. That day, however, everything was wonderful, peaceful, not an angry word was exchanged between the two of you. We went into a store that sold souvenirs and postcards to tourists. You bought him a green hat with a chamois tail. He was happy. He shoved it right on his head, it sat crooked on his curls. He might have been spoiled but he could also be happy with so little. He started singing in the car. It was a song his father used to sing. It used to bug me because it made me think of his father, who

I wasn't getting along with at the time. But I was so happy that day and all the bitterness seemed fluffy, sweet, airy. The song went:

> *Non avemo ni canones*
> *Ni tanks ni aviones*
> *Ay Carmelà*

You knew the song and started singing along:

> *El terror de los fascistas*
> *Rumba*
> *Larumba*
> *Larumba*
> *là*

It may seem stupid to have written you this letter in order to thank you for singing that day with Michele and for buying him a hat with a chamois tail that he wore for another two, maybe three, years. But I also wanted to ask you a favor. Do you know all the words to the song and if you do would you transcribe them and send them to me. It probably seems weird, but a person does fixate on simple and weird urges when the truth is she desires nothing.

Adriana

41

ADA AND ELISABETTA left for London. Osvaldo was going to fetch them from there in early September. In the meantime there were things to do at the shop. It was the twentieth of August and Angelica was going on a road trip with Oreste, the baby, and the Bettoias. Viola was staying with Adriana. The twins were going to sleepaway camp in the Dolomites.

Angelica and Viola had driven Ada and Elisabetta to the airport in Viola's car and were on their way back. Osvaldo was following in his Fiat.

That morning Angelica and Viola had gone to a notary with Lillino and signed the deed to sell the tower to the pelican. He didn't show up in person but sent a proxy to the notary. He was still in Chianti. He had a variety of ailments, Osvaldo said, each one more imaginary than the next and yet each as painful. He didn't leave his villa in Chianti anymore. Ada was running the publishing house. She managed the whole thing and didn't take a cent. But Ada couldn't have cared less about money, Angelica explained to Viola, who was driving and keeping her eyes on the road, steady and elegant. Despite the dreadful heat, her hair was perfumed and wet, well brushed, and very shiny. She wore a white linen dress, perfectly ironed and fresh. Angelica wore jeans and a ratty shirt. She'd spent the afternoon packing suitcases. She was leaving the next day.

Ada didn't care about the money, Angelica said. She couldn't care less because she had so much. The pelican didn't care about money either because he had so much. No one understood why he had bought the tower. He was never going to go there. He hadn't even seen it. Ada must have persuaded him that it was a good investment. Ada wanted to transform the tower into something, it wasn't clear what, maybe a restaurant or retirement home. "Sublimely restful," said Viola. "The tower is hard to get to. You never saw it but I went there," she said. "But I'm telling you that Ada can transform it," said Angelica. "She'll put in a road. A swimming pool. Bungalows. And I don't know what else." What brought Ada and the pelican together, observed Angelica, was their fascination with money and the transformative powers of money, along with a profound indifference to spending it and having it, while also having a great quantity of it. What made them different was that Ada couldn't imagine herself poor and she didn't even try. Instead the pelican spent his life imagining himself poor in a way that sent shivers up his spine and made him shake with horror and desire.

"That's the end of our tower," said Viola.

"It was never ours," said Angelica.

"It wasn't even that pretty," said Viola.

"I don't imagine it was," said Angelica.

"From the outside, it's a pile of stones with a window way up high. It's shaped vaguely like a tower, but you can call any pile of stones a tower if that's the name it wants to go by. Inside it smells like shit, and there is shit everywhere. I remember that more than anything else, the shit."

"But he doesn't smell," said Angelica.

"Who?"

"The pelican. He has that nose but can't smell anything."

"Anyway, we don't know why he bought it. And we don't know why our father bought it."

"If Ada told him it was a good investment, no doubt Ada is right."

"Then I don't understand why we sold it," said Viola.

"Because Lillino advised us to."

"What if he gave us bad advice?"

"We'll manage."

"I didn't know what to do with a tower of shit. On the other hand, our father bought it. I'm sorry I called it a tower of shit. I wasn't thinking. But we can't do anything about it now. The matter of the tower is closed."

"As if the matter were ever open," said Angelica.

"It's so upsetting to be alone with Mamma in that lonely house," said Viola. "I don't like lonely places. That's another reason I didn't like the tower."

"Matilde is there," said Angelica.

"Matilde's presence doesn't give me any relief at all."

"There's a telephone. Remember, there's a phone now. It's been there a week. Thanks to Ada. And Ada's dog will be there too. Osvaldo is bringing it."

"I can't stand dogs," said Viola. "I'll have to look after the dog, the rabbits, the twins' goat that needs feeding from a bottle. They should have at least taken the goat with them."

"To overnight camp?"

"I'm worried I'm pregnant," said Viola. "I'm very late."

"That's a good thing. You're always saying you want a baby."

"I'm worried about being in that remote house with no doctor nearby."

"You can call Doctor Bobo. He'll come right over. What's

the alternative anyway? Mamma can't stay there alone. Matilde sleeps very deeply. An earthquake wouldn't wake her. Cloti is on vacation. I have to go away for a few days. I promised the baby. I'll come back soon though and then you can leave."

"I know. I'm not arguing with that. I just wanted to tell you that I was worried. I wanted to say it. I don't know why you have to get on my case. I just wanted to say it. Elio left for Holland yesterday. He was dying to go by himself."

"He could've stayed with you."

"He wanted to see Holland. He needed a distraction. Poor Elio, Michele's death really got him. He's sorry we didn't go to Leeds when Michele got married. He says he could have given him good advice."

"What kind of advice?"

"I don't know. Advice. Elio is very human."

"Michele was murdered. I wonder what kind of advice he could have possibly gotten that would have protected him from the fascists who killed him."

"If he'd just stayed safe and sound in Leeds they wouldn't have killed him."

"It's possible that he found it hard to stay safe and sound."

"The last time I saw him was in Largo Argentina," said Viola. "He was coming out of the rotisserie. He said 'hello' to me and then turned away. I asked him what he'd gotten and he said, 'a roast chicken.' Those are the last words he said to me. Such nothing words. I watched him walk away with his paperback. A stranger."

They were in front of their mother's house. Viola parked the car between the two dwarf spruces, withered and drooping in the heat. Angelica pulled her suitcase down from the roof rack. "How much stuff did you bring?" said Angelica. "A roast chicken," said Viola. "I can still hear the words coming out of his mouth. We loved each other so much when we were little. We played dolls, mommy and baby. I played the mother and he played the daughter. He wanted to be the little girl. He wanted to be just like me. Then we got older and he didn't like it anymore. He resented me. He said I was bourgeois. But what else am I supposed to be. He loved you best. I was so jealous. You have so many more memories with him. You used to see him all the time. You were friends with his friends. All I knew were their names. Gianni. Anselmo. Oliviero. Osvaldo. I never liked his friendship with Osvaldo. It was a homosexual friendship. There's no use trying to hide it. You can tell just by looking at him. And Elio told me that he'd seen them together. I still don't know how I feel about Michele becoming a homosexual. Michele would call me a conformist. It's unnerving to see Osvaldo. He's sweet and everything but it upsets me to see him. He comes over here a lot so I'm going to see him a lot. Why does he come here? Who knows. And here he is, driving up. I recognize the sound of his Fiat. But Mamma likes it. Or maybe she never thought about it. Or maybe she thought about it and got used to it. You can get used to anything, probably."

"You can get used to anything when there's nothing else left," said Angelica.

42

September 8, 1971—Leeds

Dear Angelica,

I got to Leeds yesterday morning. I stayed in a boardinghouse called the Hong-Kong. You can't imagine anything sadder than the Hong-Kong boardinghouse in Leeds.

Ada and Elisabetta stayed on in London because there was no reason for them to come along.

I tracked down that boy who wrote you, Ermanno Giustiniani. He's at the same address he gave you. He's a nice boy, sharp face, pale, almost sickly. He told me that his mother has Asiatic origins.

He told me that Eileen and the children have gone back to America. He doesn't have their address. He told me that Eileen is a very intelligent woman and a drunk. Michele married her with the idea that he would save her from alcohol. That sounds just like him. He loved to be called on to help his neighbor. But his generosity was useless because he couldn't stick it out. Their marriage was in ruins by the eighth day. They were happy for eight days. Ermanno didn't know them during those days, he met them after, when the marriage was practically over. But friends told him that for eight days Eileen had stopped drinking and seemed like a different person.

Ermanno took me to the house on Nelson Road where Eileen and Michele lived. There was a "For Sale" sign on the house. I asked the estate agents if I could see it. A little English house with three floors, a piano room furnished with sordid, faux-liberty furniture. I went through every room. There was an apron in the kitchen that might have been Eileen's. There was a tomato and carrot pattern on it, and there was a raincoat that might have been hers too, shiny black with a rip in the sleeve. But I'm just guessing. In one room there was a bowl with sour milk in it on the ground, obviously left for a cat, and pictures on the walls of Snow White and the seven dwarfs. I'm describing all of this in such detail because I think you'll want to know. I couldn't find anything of Michele's except a wool undershirt for winter weather, the label says it's from Anticoli on Via della Vita. I felt uncertain for a moment and then left it where it was. I don't think there's any point in preserving things that used to belong to the dead once they've been handled by strangers and the identity has evaporated.

Visiting this house, I feel like I'm drowning in endless melancholy. Now I'm back in my room at the boardinghouse and can see the city of Leeds through the window, one of the last cities Michele walked through. I'm having dinner with Ermanno Giustiniani tonight and he's a nice boy but he can't tell me much about Michele because he didn't know him for that long and doesn't remember much, or perhaps it makes him sad to talk about it with me. He's a boy. Boys today don't have big memories, and more importantly, they don't cultivate their memories. You know Michele didn't have much in the way of memories, maybe he never went out of his way to cultivate them. You and your mother have a stronger inclination to preserve memories. This life now has nothing to equal to the places and moments we passed through to get here. I've lived things and observed things, knowing all the while that each moment had extraordinary splendor. I had to make myself remember. It was always so painful to me that Michele didn't want to, or couldn't, understand such splendor, that he moved forward without ever turning back. But I believe he sensed my splendor. A number of times I have thought that maybe while he was dying he had a flash of understanding and he traveled all the paths of his memory and I am consoled by this thought because nothing brings consolation when there is nothing left, and even seeing that dusty undershirt in that kitchen, and then leaving it behind, was a strange, icy, lonely consolation.

Osvaldo

New Directions Paperbooks—a partial listing

Federico García Lorca, Selected Poems*
  Three Tragedies
Nathaniel Mackey, Splay Anthem
Xavier de Maistre, Voyage Around My Room
Stéphane Mallarmé, Selected Poetry and Prose*
Javier Marías, Your Face Tomorrow (3 volumes)
Harry Mathews, The Solitary Twin
Bernadette Mayer, Works & Days
Carson McCullers, The Member of the Wedding
Thomas Merton, New Seeds of Contemplation
  The Way of Chuang Tzu
Henri Michaux, A Barbarian in Asia
Dunya Mikhail, The Beekeeper
Henry Miller, The Colossus of Maroussi
  Big Sur & the Oranges of Hieronymus Bosch
Yukio Mishima, Confessions of a Mask
  Death in Midsummer
  Star
Eugenio Montale, Selected Poems*
Vladimir Nabokov, Laughter in the Dark
  Nikolai Gogol
  The Real Life of Sebastian Knight
Raduan Nassar, A Cup of Rage
Pablo Neruda, The Captain's Verses*
  Love Poems*
Charles Olson, Selected Writings
George Oppen, New Collected Poems
Wilfred Owen, Collected Poems
Michael Palmer, The Laughter of the Sphinx
Nicanor Parra, Antipoems*
Boris Pasternak, Safe Conduct
Kenneth Patchen
  Memoirs of a Shy Pornographer
Octavio Paz, Poems of Octavio Paz
Victor Pelevin, Omon Ra
Alejandra Pizarnik
  Extracting the Stone of Madness
Ezra Pound, The Cantos
  New Selected Poems and Translations
Raymond Queneau, Exercises in Style
Qian Zhongshu, Fortress Besieged
Raja Rao, Kanthapura
Herbert Read, The Green Child
Kenneth Rexroth, Selected Poems
Keith Ridgway, Hawthorn & Child
Rainer Maria Rilke
  Poems from the Book of Hours
Arthur Rimbaud, Illuminations*
  A Season in Hell and The Drunken Boat*

Guillermo Rosales, The Halfway House
Evelio Rosero, The Armies
Fran Ross, Oreo
Joseph Roth, The Emperor's Tomb
  The Hotel Years
Raymond Roussel, Locus Solus
Ihara Saikaku, The Life of an Amorous Woman
Nathalie Sarraute, Tropisms
Jean-Paul Sartre, Nausea
  The Wall
Delmore Schwartz
  In Dreams Begin Responsibilities
Hasan Shah, The Dancing Girl
W. G. Sebald, The Emigrants
  The Rings of Saturn
  Vertigo
Stevie Smith, Best Poems
Gary Snyder, Turtle Island
Muriel Spark, The Driver's Seat
  The Girls of Slender Means
  Memento Mori
Reiner Stach, Is That Kafka?
Antonio Tabucchi, Pereira Maintains
Junichiro Tanizaki, A Cat, a Man & Two Women
Yoko Tawada, The Emissary
  Memoirs of a Polar Bear
Dylan Thomas, A Child's Christmas in Wales
  Collected Poems
Uwe Timm, The Invention of Curried Sausage
Tomas Tranströmer
  The Great Enigma: New Collected Poems
Leonid Tsypkin, Summer in Baden-Baden
Frederic Tuten, The Adventures of Mao
Regina Ullmann, The Country Road
Paul Valéry, Selected Writings
Enrique Vila-Matas, Bartleby & Co.
Elio Vittorini, Conversations in Sicily
Rosmarie Waldrop, Gap Gardening
Robert Walser, The Assistant
  The Tanners
Eliot Weinberger, The Ghosts of Birds
Nathanael West, The Day of the Locust
  Miss Lonelyhearts
Tennessee Williams, Cat on a Hot Tin Roof
  The Glass Menagerie
  A Streetcar Named Desire
William Carlos Williams, Selected Poems
  Spring and All
Louis Zukofsky, "A"

*BILINGUAL EDITION

For a complete listing, request a free catalog from New Directions, 80 8th Avenue, New York, NY 10011 or visit us online at **ndbooks.com**